YOUR *Heart* IS MINE

2

A Criminal Romance

A NOVEL BY

VIVIAN

D1410133

CHAPTER ONE

$\mathcal{T}$he funeral was over, and everyone had gone back to their cars. The limos were waiting, but Big Lee and Lay were still seated in their chairs, staring at Cam's coffin. They both had taken his death hard, and at one point, Whisper had to escort Big Lee out of the church during the service. She blamed herself for the demise of her little brother. If she hadn't agreed to help Cecil, this would have never happened to Cameron.

"Come on, baby. It's time to go," Whisper cooed. He put his hand on Big Lee's shoulder and gripped it firmly. She continued to stare at the coffin because she wasn't ready to leave just yet.

"I'm not ready to go," Big Lee stated calmly. "I just can't leave him here all by himself. This here is final, Whisper, and I can't bear to go." Big Lee squeezed Lay's hand because neither one of them wanted to say goodbye. Big Lee was always by her little brother's side, and when Cam was younger, he'd gotten his appendix taken out. Big Lee, along with Lay as an infant, stayed up at the hospital from the time Cam was checked in, and they didn't leave until he was released.

"Ann, the people at the cemetery need us to leave so they can put him in the ground. As long as you're sitting there, they can't do their job," Whisper explained.

"It's my money that paid for him to be put here, so they can wait until I'm ready to leave!" Big Lee insisted. "I'll pay the muthafuckas overtime if money is what they're worried about!"

"It's not about the money, baby. They have another funeral coming in a few minutes, and they need to get this ready for the next family," Whisper uttered sternly. He understood that his baby was in a lot of pain, but she needed to come on and let these people do their job. Big Lee looked up at Whisper with tears in her eyes.

"This is the final goodbye, and I just can't let him go!" Big Lee cried uncontrollably. Lay let her mother's hand go and got up out of the chair. She walked up to Cam's casket and placed her face on top of it. She spread her arms around it as far as they would go and closed her eyes, hoping and wishing that Cam would just get up out of it. She'd been having nightmares from seeing his bullet-riddled body on the floor of the garage, but she never said anything to anyone, because she didn't want to burden them. Reed had been very supportive of her at this time of bereavement, but she didn't feel truly connected to him, and felt he couldn't understand the issues that came along with being in a family like hers.

"Lee Ann Michelle! Get up and let's go!" her mother snapped firmly. Whisper and Big Lee turned to see Mrs. Wilson standing a few feet from them. "You are allowed to grieve your brother's death, but you can do it in the comfort of your own home! These people need to go on with their day, and you sitting here holding up progress is ridiculous!" Lee Ann's father walked up to her and grabbed her hand.

Next, he pulled her up from her chair and wrapped his arms around his daughter.

"Come on, baby girl," said Mr. Wilson, rocking them. "I know this hurts, but you have to be strong for your brothers and the girls. You are the glue that holds everyone together, and if you fall apart, how is everything going to continue to function?"

"I guess you're right, Daddy, but this hurts so bad!" Big Lee sobbed. "You know Cam was my shadow, and I don't know what I'm going to do now that he's dead! He used to come over my house every morning to see me. What is Tamara going to do now that she has to raise their baby by herself?" Cam's wife, Tamara, was seven months pregnant, and he was excited about becoming a father.

"We're going to support her like the Wilson family does, and make sure that his unborn child knows about their father," Mr. Wilson assured her. "Now come on, baby, and let's go." Mr. Wilson looked over at Whisper. "Can you go get my grandbaby, please?"

"Yes, sir," Whisper replied. He looked at Lee Ann with sorrow in his eyes then walked off to get Lay.

"Come on, baby girl." Whisper sighed. "Your grandfather sent me over here to get you." Lay continued to hug on the top of the casket, because her heart was truly hurting. Cam was like the big brother she never had, and Big Lee raised them to be that way. He was the one who always looked out for her and made sure that she was squared away. They were five years apart, and he was always over Big Lee's house with them. That's why people often wondered if Cam was really Big Lee's son. He was the one who taught Lay how to drive, told her about niggas, and bought Lay her first gun on her eighteenth birthday. He showed her how to use it, and made sure every birthday after that one, a new hammer was added to her collection. "I know this is the first major death for you, Lay. It's never easy, but you have to find some way to move on."

"How can I move on when Cam was a big part of my everyday life?" Lay questioned. "No one's going to take care of me like Cam."

"I can't take care of you like Cam, baby girl. But I can be there for you like a father and fuck a muthafucka up if he trips with you, like Cam." Lay sat up and stared at Whisper for second, amused. A sliver of a smile came across her face, even though she felt so badly.

"You would do that anyway, Whisper," Lay replied, wiping tears away.

"Layloni! We're leaving," called out her grandfather.

"Yes, sir," Lay replied solemnly with a sad look on her face. Whisper held his hand out to Lay, and she quickly grabbed it like she did when she was a little girl on her way to the store with her godfather. He squeezed it tightly, then held it up to his lips and kissed the back of it. Next, he led them off toward the limo, and they followed behind Big Lee and Mr. Wilson. Byrd sat in his car and watched Lay from a distance as they waited for the limos to leave so that they could pull off. He wanted to be by Lay's side the moment he'd heard what happened, but her new little friend seemed to always be around, and it made Byrd keep his distance. This angered him because he knew he should be the one there comforting Layloni. He had forgiven her for stabbing him in the leg the day after the incident happened, but he was still mad at her for the simple fact that she claimed they jumped her when it wasn't anything like that. He wanted to reach out to let her know that he still cared, even with all the tension between them. Byrd had some things he wanted to discuss with her, and his visit with Cam the day before his death was one of the things they needed to talk about. Byrd couldn't believe that Cam was gone, and he wished that there was something he could do to help avenge his death. More importantly, he wished that he could have a moment of Lay's time so that he could express his condolences in person.

Cam had gone to visit Byrd because he wanted to make sure that Byrd wasn't going to try to hurt his niece. He felt like it was unfortunate that things got out of hand between Byrd and Lay, and he wanted to see if there was any way for a reconciliation between them. Byrd assured Cam that he wasn't going to cause harm to Lay. He confessed his love to Cam for her and explained how he still wanted to be her man. Byrd figured if he told Cam the issue behind their breakup, and how he figured if Lay saw him with someone else, she would get her act together and come claim him as her own. Cam told Byrd that he was stupid for the shit he'd done and caused himself the strife that he was facing. Also, Cam told Byrd that he only caused a bigger wedge between him and Lay, because Lay would rather leave him alone than to deal with the bullshit of dick and pussy issues. He went on to explain to Byrd how he stressed to Lay not to be dependent upon a nigga. He talked about how Big Lee raised Lay, and how daughters tended to follow in their mother's footsteps. By the time Cam and Byrd finished their talk, Byrd had a better understanding of Lay and the way her mind worked. It was easy for her to pick out the fault in her mother's actions, but she found it difficult in accepting the fact that she was doing the same thing.

Byrd watched as Reed walked up to Lay and Whisper. He noticed Lay's body language, and it didn't seem she was feeling Reed by the way she continued to hold on to Whisper's hand as they walked to the car. Reed tried to take Lay's hand away, but she wouldn't budge. Byrd longed to go be by Lay's side. He wanted to hold her and take all the pain away, because he felt like that was his job. He made a promise to Cam that he would try to work things out with Lay. Cam told him not to worry about that other nigga that's sniffing at Lay's skirt because he wasn't her type anyway. However, Cam felt that Byrd was the best person for his niece, and he was going to make sure that the two of them got back together.

"That's fucked up how Geechie and 'em did Killa Cam," ManMan mumbled. "He was a stand-up dude and never fucked with anyone."

"Yeah, Cam was my cat," Byrd agreed. "But a dope fiend is always looking for a way to get something off on a muthafucka."

"You know he approached me about getting in on the robbery, but I turned his ass down!" ManMan scoffed. "I'm glad I told his ass that I wasn't interested. Who'd a thought the nigga wanted to rob the Wilsons? Only a stupid muthafucka would do something that dumb!"

"Agreed," Byrd replied, staring out of the window at Lay. "Cam had come to talk to me about some shit the day before he died." ManMan chuckled a little.

"He must have come to smooth things over with you about that shit with Lay," ManMan speculated.

"Something like that," Byrd replied. "I ain't tripping off that shit with Lay, because I shouldn't have grabbed her in the first place. I know she's crazy as hell, and I should have just let her beat the shit out of Shakey." ManMan looked at Byrd, confused. He and Byrd were smoking a blunt, and ManMan thought the weed was getting to Byrd's brain.

"Dude! That bitch stabbed you, and you had to get thirty stitches! I wouldn't be so cool about it!" ManMan insisted. Byrd looked over at ManMan, smugly.

"But you ain't me," Byrd replied. "Do you know why Lay beat up Shakey?"

"Naw," ManMan replied. "That's the million-dollar question on everyone's mind!" Byrd looked at his best friend for a moment, feeling some type of way. He wondered if he should let ManMan in on the truth, or should he leave him out in the dark. "Do you know something, Byrd?"

"Naw, ManMan, I don't know shit. However, my suspicions were that Lay was jealous because she saw me and Shakey rocking together. You know Lay saw Shakey giving me some head at the gambling house the day she came to get her earrings."

"Damn, but, dude... Why would Lay give a fuck about you and Shakey being together?" ManMan scoffed and laughed. "You and Lay barely talked to each other, so that doesn't make sense!" Byrd looked at ManMan stupidly with his lips turned up.

"Why do you think, dumb ass? Lay was my straight fuckin' gal, and the reason why we didn't talk much in public was because we were fucking around on the low. She's still my bitch, even though shit went wrong between us, but for the past year and a half, I've been knocking the bottom out of that pussy!" Byrd explained. "Why do you think she

7

kept shooting you down?" ManMan looked at Byrd in disbelief for a minute.

"Nigga, you're lying!" ManMan shouted and laughed heartily. "Ain't no way Lay was fucking with you for a little over a year, nigga, and no one knew about it! Any man that had Lay on his arm would proudly show that thang off!"

"Not if that's against what she wanted," Byrd rebutted. "Don't you think I would have paraded Lay in front of you niggas if I could have? Lay ain't down for the public displays of affection, and that's the reason why we going through this short separation."

"Man, you're lying!" ManMan insisted. "'Cause if that was the case, why has she been all up on that nigga that's been hanging around her, here and now lately? You know the one I told you about from the gas station. I've seen them out and shit, and her Facebook page and Snap has been poppin' with pics of them." Byrd looked at ManMan annoyed, because he'd been seeing the posts too. He knew that Lay was doing it on purpose, because she never posted no niggas on her page except her family. But that nigga Reed wasn't talking about shit. None of that social media bullshit mattered, because he was going to get his boo back, and soon.

"Watch what I tell you, nigga… She's going to be back with daddy soon enough."

"And she's going to do a threesome up in my house with us," ManMan cracked sarcastically.

"Nigga, you better watch your mouth!" Byrd snapped. "Don't talk about my bitch like that, because I find that very disrespectful!" ManMan looked at Byrd in disbelief.

"Whatever, Byrd," ManMan scoffed. "And I guess you're going to tell me that Big Lee was the one who gave you all that dope, too!" Byrd looked over at ManMan with a smirk on his face.

"She didn't, but that's none of your business," Byrd assured him.

CHAPTER TWO

$\mathcal{T}$hree weeks had passed since Geechie's crew killed Cam. Today was the funeral, and Geechie was held up in Angie's apartment, scared to death. Word had gotten back to him that one of his guys that was in on the robbery, was found dead. That didn't count the man that was left in the garage, and from what someone else told him, they found his mans J.J. hanging from a tree at Tandy's park. Someone had hung him upside down by his legs and beat him like a piñata with a baseball bat. This type of display was a clear message to Geechie that the Wilson's weren't playing with any of them, and death was truly certain for him and anyone else who had something to do with Cam's death.

"He's been held up in the basement since he got here a week ago," Angie explained. "He comes upstairs to eat, shit, shave, and bathe, but as soon as he's done, he goes right back downstairs."

"I hear that Big Lee and her brothers are on a warpath," Cecil mentioned. "Word around here is that if they can't find Geechie, they're going to put a hit out on me."

"Do you think that's going to happen?" Angie uttered, sounding worried. "I mean, you didn't have anything to do with the bullshit.

Geechie acted on his own dumb ass merit."

"I know, baby, but he's my little brother. I was the one who had Geechie representing me and going to pick up the packages. I know Lee can't possibly think that I had anything to do with the robbery," Cecil speculated. "She knows me better than that, and why would I send my brother to rob her if I was trying to get back with her?"

"Wait! You were trying to get back with her?" Angie repeated. She'd caught an attitude real quick, because she'd been the one busting her ass for Cecil.

"Don't go jumping to conclusions, Angie. You're my ride or die, but if I could have convinced Big Lee to take me back, I could have funneled money and dope to you, while we continued to build our thing." Angie wasn't buying what Cecil was selling. If Big Lee allowed Cecil to come back into her life, there's no way he would ever leave that much money and power.

"You must think I'm a fool because I'm young," Angie scoffed. "I know you wouldn't leave Big Lee for me! I ain't stupid, Cecil."

"I don't think you're a fool or stupid, baby. Also, I know that Big Lee has made it known that she and Whisper is a couple, now. They've been seen out in public being affectionate, and she even told one of my homeboys that we're no longer married," Cecil scoffed. "That bitch has some big nuts!"

"She's doing what any woman would do when she's ready to move on with their life," Angie co-signed. "She's been done with you a long time ago, and now with Geechie killing Cam, that put the nail in the coffin." Angie's phone vibrated, letting her know she had a text message.

She pulled the phone from her face and saw it was from Ax. She put the phone on speaker so she could check it. "What do you want me to tell your brother?"

Text Message (Ax): Where you at? I need to see you, bad!

Angie smiled because she wanted to see Ax too. They'd been sneaking around for the past few months. She'd given him a fake name and called herself Amanda.

"Did you hear what I said to you, Angie?" Cecil snapped.

"My fault, Cecil. I missed all of it," Angie apologized. "I thought I heard some movement downstairs, so I wasn't paying attention."

"Are you sure everything is cool over there?" Cecil asked, skeptically.

"Yeah. everything's cool," Angie assured him. "But I think your brother needs to hit it out of town, because all of his accomplices are dead." Cecil held the phone for a moment, not knowing what to say. Geechie should have known better than to go against the grain, and this time, he'd fucked up royally!

"I agree," Cecil replied. "Can you take him the phone?" Angie sighed as she rolled her eyes up in her head.

"You know that me and that dude don't get along!" Angie fussed. "He keeps trying to fuck me after I told him I wasn't interested. He knows that I'm your gal, so why is he trippin'?"

"I'll speak to him about that shit too," Cecil assured her. "Can you please take him the phone, baby. I'll talk to Geechie and tell him that he has to leave your house today. Does that work for you?" Cecil begged.

"I guess, Cecil, but I want his ass gone like yesterday!" Angie spat. "And even if you don't tell him to go, I'll make sure that he gets his shit and leave!"

"What yo' tough ass gon' do?" Cecil teased and laughed.

"That's for me to know, and for you to find out," Angie scoffed. She walked to the basement door and opened it. "Geechie! Cecil wants to holla at you!" There was silence for a moment then she heard him coming up the stairs. She took a few steps back as Geechie emerged through the door. He was a squatty man, but his body was solid. His gut hung over his pants, but his arms were muscular and stacked. His skin was dark brown, and he always had stubble on his face. He almost put you in the mind of a hound dog by his facial features, and he kept his head shaved bald.

"Damn, Angie! Those jeans are tight as fuck!" said Geechie, lustfully eyeing her. "Why don't you let me peel you out of them joints after I get off the phone with my brother?" Angie handed Geechie the phone as she glared at him vehemently.

"After you get off the phone with your brother, your dusty ass will be leaving my house!" Angie declared angrily. "Now hurry the fuck up, because I got shit to do!" Angie turned and walked away from him because the sight of him made her sick. Geechie grinned at Angie as she disappeared out of the kitchen. His dick was semi hard from watching her ass jiggle when she stormed out of the room. He was convinced that he was going to have to take the pussy, because she wasn't going to give it up voluntarily.

"Hello," Geechie grumbled.

"You're real disrespectful, dumb nigga!" Cecil hissed. "First you take from my wife, and now you're making advances at my bitch while I'm on the phone! What the fuck is up with you?"

"Ain't shit up with me, Cecil. I was just playing with that bitch! She always got a fucking attitude," Geechie complained.

"You're lucky that you're my brother, because I swear to God—"

"You swear to God, what, Cecil? You ain't gon' do shit, and you know it! Your ass is soft as cotton and won't bust a grape if another nigga was pressing yo' fingers!" Geechie retorted and laughed.

"I'm glad you're feeling tough, Geechie, but we both know the deal. If I was out there on them streets, yo' ass wouldn't be talking all that tough shit! Pack your shit up and move the crowd, bitch ass nigga!" Cecil ordered. "Ain't nobody going to keep harboring your disrespectful ass!"

"What the fuck you mean?" Geechie snapped. "Where the fuck am I supposed to go?"

"If you're smart, you'll take your ass to Chicago and lay low until I get out in a few months," Cecil replied. "You know that Big Lee and her brothers are looking for you. I heard they got ahold of your boy and strung his ass up! Said they beat him until his head busted open like a melon."

"I… I… saw the pictures," Geechie stuttered. "But I wasn't in the garage when Cam got killed. I was waiting in the car!"

"But they knew your dumb ass set it up! I told you that I had shit under control, and then you had to go and do some stupid shit like that. What the fuck were you thinking… my fault, you weren't!"

"Aye, look here!" Geechie insisted, frowning. "Tell your bitch to give me a few dollars and I'll leave. She took the bag of dope from me and hid it."

"Like I told her to," Cecil replied. "Now give Angie back the phone so I can give her instructions." Geechie turned to find Angie standing in the doorway. She had on her coat with her hands in the pockets.

"My brother wants to speak back to you," Geechie said as he seethed. Angie walked over to Geechie and took the phone. "I guess it was your idea to have me leave."

"Whatever," Angie uttered with an attitude. "Hello."

"Give that nigga some money so he can get out of town," Cecil ordered.

"How much you want me to give him?" asked Angie, annoyed.

"Give his ass about a grand," Cecil instructed. "That should hold him over for a while."

"And if it doesn't?" Angie questioned boldly.

"Then his ass gon' be shit out of luck!" Cecil scoffed. "I appreciate everything that you're doing, Angie. Your efforts won't go unrewarded." Angie chuckled a little.

"Yeah… we'll see. I'll talk to you later," Angie replied sarcastically.

"I love you, smart ass!" Cecil cooed. "Talk to you later."

"Ditto!" Angie replied. She hung up the phone and stared at Geechie, displeased. She felt like he was an appendage that would constantly be a problem. "Take this money, get your shit, and let's go!" She reached into her pocket and pulled out a wad of cash.

16

"You cut straight to the chase, don't you?" Geechie smirked. "What? You don't like having me in your house?" He walked up on Angie, and she quickly pulled out her hammer. "Damn! You're pulling out guns and shit on me? Do I make you nervous?" Geechie rubbed his nose to clear his sinuses.

"You don't make me nervous. I just don't trust your ass," Angie replied, smugly. She held out the money, and Geechie snatched it out of her hand.

"Don't think that I don't know you're playing my brother," Geechie mentioned casually. "But that's on his stupid ass! However, I don't understand how he fell for a bitch he ain't never smashed."

"It ain't none of your damn business! Now get your shit and get the fuck up out of my house!" Angie retorted firmly. Geechie smirked as he walked away.

"You know this ain't over," Geechie uttered. "I'll see you again!"

"And I dread to see that day come!"

CHAPTER THREE

$\mathcal{B}$yrd walked into Tandy's Community Center where Cam's repast was being held. He went home to change clothes and get his wares for the day. He took it down to his new dope spot on Walton before he went to continue paying his respects to the Wilsons. He'd helped an old acquaintance, and she told him he could set up shop in her apartment. At first Byrd was skeptical, because he thought she was trying to get over on him. However, when he met her girlfriend, he figured it just might work out.

Byrd walked into the gymnasium where everyone was gathered. There were rows of tables and chairs set out where people were seated, eating and socializing. He looked around to see if he could spot Lay, but the only people he saw from her family that he recognized were Craig, Ralph, Rico, Deacon, and Ax. He wasn't surprised that Big Lee wasn't in attendance. She'd been real low key since her brother's death, and word on the street was that she didn't want to be around anyone but her immediate family.

"Byrd, come here," called out his mother, Tabitha.

"Yes, ma'am," he replied, holding up his finger. He walked over to the table where she was serving food and kissed her on the cheek.

"What's up, Mama?"

"I need for you to take these bags of food over to Lee Ann's house so that she and Layloni can eat," Tabitha instructed. Byrd looked at her blankly. "What? I know you're not still tripping off what happened between you and Lay? You told me you forgave her."

"Naw, Mama, it's all good. I was just thinking about something else," Byrd offered. "I ain't got no problems taking this to them." Tabitha looked at her son skeptically.

"Okay, baby," she replied. "Let me finish wrapping them up some cake and then you can be on your way."

"A'ight, Mama," Byrd replied nonchalantly. This might be his opportunity to express his condolences to Lay personally. He'd already spoken to Big Lee, and it was hurtful to see her in so much pain.

Byrd pulled up in front of Big Lee's house and turned off his ignition. There were a few cars lined up down the block, but Lay's car wasn't one of them. He figured she might be at her house, so he made a mental note to go by there when he was done delivering the food. He walked up to the door and rang the bell. He stepped back, because he didn't want to seem anxious or anything. Whisper opened the door and smiled as they stared at each other.

"What's up, Byrd Man?" asked Whisper in a chipper voice.

"You got it," Byrd replied. He held up the bags in his hands. "My mama sent you guys some food."

"Okay. Come on in," Whisper offered, stepping out of the way. Byrd walked into the house and noticed no one was there but Whisper and Big Lee. Big Lee looked over in Byrd's direction and smiled warmly.

"Hey sweetie," said Big Lee softly. "What do you have there?"

"My mama sent you guys some food. She said to tell you that she'll be by later to make sure you ate something," Byrd explained. "I'm not gon' tell you what else she said out of respect." Big Lee chuckled a little, because Tabitha had been fussing at her for not eating since all of the chaos happened.

"I love your mama," Big Lee replied and smiled. "That's my bestie, and she always has my back!"

"She says you're her sister, and she has to make sure you're alright, because you always do it for everyone else," Byrd replied. "Where do you want me to put it?" Big Lee got up from the couch.

"Let's put it in the kitchen," she answered. "I need to go upstairs, and wake Lay up to come eat. She hasn't had much of an appetite since Cam died, and all she does is sleep." Byrd looked down at the floor then back up at Big Lee, sadly. "Have you talked to my baby?" Big Lee took the bags out of his hands and put them on the counter. "Have a seat, Byrd."

"I can't stay," Byrd uttered nonchalantly. "I have something to do." Big Lee smirked at him.

"You don't have to worry," Big Lee assured him. "Reed is gone back overseas. Besides, he doesn't know what to do with my baby. She didn't even want him around most of the time." Big Lee and Whisper laughed. "She kept sending him away every time he came over, and I started to feel sorry for the poor boy. His intentions were pure, but you know my baby. If she ain't trying to be bothered, then she ain't gone be bothered!"

"Well they sure seemed chummy at the burial," Byrd pointed out. Big Lee cut her eyes at Byrd.

"That's because he was saying goodbye to her. He was about to leave for the airport when we were walking to the cars," Big Lee explained. She looked at Byrd and saw the jealousy written all over his face. "Let me share something with you, baby. My daughter is in love with you and only you! She grieved after she stabbed you, and I was the one who had to listen to her cries. See, you played a dangerous game by messing with my baby's heart. You got the end result you weren't looking for when you called yourself teaching her a lesson, but any man would have told you not to do the stupid shit that you did in the first place."

"I wasn't trying to do nothing, Big Lee," Byrd scoffed, defensively.

"I can't tell, lil' nigga," Whisper interjected. "'Cause you knew that Lay was going to be pissed about you fucking with Shakey!" Byrd gave both of them a guilty look. "Now the way I see it, you can either keep sitting here with me and Ann like a dumb nigga, or you can go upstairs and check on Lay." Byrd looked down at his hands then back up at Whisper.

"Gone 'head," Big Lee added and smiled. "She's asleep in my room." Byrd hesitated for a moment then he got up out of his chair. "It takes a strong man to forgive his woman when she does something to harm him, both physically and emotionally; but if you love my daughter, you'll find a way to move past this, and it will make your bond stronger." Byrd stared at both of them blankly. He didn't know what else to say, so he headed toward the steps to go see Lay.

Byrd stood in the doorway of Big Lee's room. Lay was fast asleep, and she looked so peaceful to him. He remembered how he used to watch her sleep and wondered would their children look like her. A warm smile came across his face as she stirred around on the bed. He walked up to it and rubbed her calf gently. Next, he climbed up on top of the mattress and rested snugly against Lay. He wrapped his arm around her waist and smelled the sweet scent of her hair. A warm and familiar comfort encompassed him as he slowly closed his eyes. This was what he longed for on those lonely nights away from her, and this is what Cam was talking about when he asked Byrd if he loved Lay. He let his thoughts carry him into slumber as he dreamed about their conversation. This is where it felt like he needed to be, and for once in his life, he realized truly what heaven felt like.

****

Lay slowly opened her eyes as the streetlights shown through the window. She'd been sleep for most of the evening and felt like she still hadn't had enough. She glanced down at an arm that was hanging off the side of her. She remembered that Reed had left for the airport, so it couldn't have possibly been him. She had been avoiding him like the plague when Cam died, and a part of her felt badly. He tried to be supportive to her, but Lay just wasn't feeling him. She longed for Byrd to show up on her doorstep, but she realized that would foolish of her, after all that had happened between them. She lifted her head and noticed a tattoo of a bald eagle on the hand attached to the arm. A sinking feeling came to Lay's stomach, because she realized who the mystery person was holding her. It was her baby, and he'd finally come to see about her.

Lay slowly turned over and stared lovingly at Byrd's sleeping face. She smiled as his familiar snores sounded like music to her ears. This was the one thing that she wanted, other than for her uncle Cam to come back to life. She knew that wasn't a reality, so at least one of her prayers had been answered.

Lay placed her hand on Byrd's cheek and sank her finger into his skin. Next, she leaned in and placed a kiss on the tip of his nose and let her lips trail down to his lips. She pressed them firmly against his and breathed in his essence. It was a smell that was etched into her senses and was committed to her brain. She stared at his eyes, until they popped open and stared back at her. At first, they displayed a look of panic, but then they turned into a look of love. Lay started to pull away, but Byrd quickly placed his hand on her back. He slid his body closer to her then placed his lips back against hers. He let his fingers slide and linger down her spine until his hands comfortably rested on her backside. Lay breathed heavily against Byrd's mouth as the moistness of her yearning began to wet her underwear.

"I'm sorry," Lay whispered urgently. "I'm sorry for—" Byrd placed his finger against Lay's lips.

"I know you are," he replied, kissing her nose. "You told me in over a hundred messages, two hundred text messages, a dozen white roses, several plants that you left outside my door, and a ton of groceries that you're going to have to prepare for me," Byrd instructed and smirked. "I don't want to talk about it, Lay, because it was both of our faults. I knew your ass was crazy as hell, so it was stupid of me to grab you. I don't know why you and Shakey were fighting, and to tell you the truth,

I don't give a fuck! I know you ain't no petty bitch, so she had to have provoked you to fight her."

Lay stared silently at Byrd as he spoke his peace. She was happy to hear that he forgave her, but she knew he would never forget.

"All I want is for us to be together, Lay. I'll even go along with the keeping it between us thing. I just want my baby back, because I truly miss my best friend."

"I missed you too, baby," Lay stammered. "I wanted you to come to me when Cam died. I tried to leave and get to you, but my mama wouldn't let me out of her sight. One night I managed to sneak out the house, but as soon as I went to pull off, Whisper was on me like a polyester suit on an old pimp's back." Byrd laughed as a smile crept across Lay's face. "I'm so glad you're here!"

"I'm glad I'm here too," Byrd admitted. "I ain't been able to sleep right since the day we parted." She looked at him nonchalantly.

"Funny... I slept like a baby." Byrd looked at Lay skeptically and grabbed her. Next, he planted a kiss firmly on her lips, and they nestled into each other's arms as they reconciled their differences.

CHAPTER FOUR

"Where's your mama?" Mrs. Wilson asked Lay aggressively.

"She's sitting in her room, listening to church music and reading the bible," Lay replied. "Grandma, I'm worried about my mama. She hasn't been herself since Cam died." Mrs. Wilson looked at Lay and pursed her lips.

"Your mother needs to stop blaming herself for what happened. She had nothing to do with any of that mess. How can you blame yourself for a robbery?" asked Mrs. Wilson confused. "That's just ridiculous to me, and since when did she and Jamal become a couple? I mean, I know he used to follow her around my house, but Lee Ann is a married woman! She shouldn't be carrying on like that."

"Carrying on like what, Mama?" Big Lee asked, walking into the room. Lay looked up and saw her mother standing in the doorway. Mrs. Wilson turned to face her daughter with a smug look on her face.

"I'm talking about you and this little circus you got going on around here with Jamal. You're a married woman, and you have your lover living in your house. What are you going to do when Cecil gets home?" Mrs. Wilson questioned nosily.

"Mama, this is exactly why I moved you clear across the country so you wouldn't meddle in matters that don't concern you," Big Lee replied defensively. She walked over to the refrigerator and opened it.

"Lee Ann, you know that I only want what is best for you and this family. I'm like that about all of my children, and you know that for a fact!" Mrs. Wilson insisted. "I love Jamal like he's one of my sons, but I thought he just had a little puppy love for you. I didn't know that this foolishness was that serious." Big Lee pulled the container of orange juice out of the refrigerator and shut the door. Next, she walked over to the cabinet and grabbed a glass out of it.

"So you mean to tell me, you didn't hear us having sex in my room for all those years?" Big Lee asked, pouring some of the juice into the glass. Mrs. Wilson cut her eyes at Big Lee and stared at her defensively.

"I... I... mean," Mrs. Wilson stuttered.

"Exactly!" Big Lee replied. Mrs. Wilson stared at Big Lee then looked over at Lay. She stared at her granddaughter for a few seconds, then her eyes widened, and her mouth dropped open with a revelation.

"Oh my God! Jamal is Layloni's father!" Mrs. Wilson blurted out. Big Lee had the glass of juice turned up to her mouth when it slipped out of her hand and hit the floor.

"Mama, what is Grandma talking about?" Lay asked, feeling confused. "Why is she saying Whisper is my father?" Big Lee stood paralyzed, because this was not how she wanted to tell Lay the truth about Whisper being her father.

"Why would you blurt something like that out?" Big Lee stammered. She was feeling anxious and conflicted, because now the cat was out of the bag.

"Because it's the truth! Jamal was always spending the night over our house, and y'all played me like I was dumb. He would sneak his ass down to your room, like I didn't know what was going on, but again, my focus was more so on those sons of mine. I guess I played naïve because your father insisted that you weren't doing anything inappropriate. However, I should have known better 'cause that pussy was hot! I should have put your ass on birth control when you were fourteen like I wanted to, but your father felt it was unnecessary," Mrs. Wilson recalled. "I got seven children, and six of them are boys. The only thing that's on a little boy's mind is being nasty, and Ralph and Rico were the worst out of all y'all; Jamal's ass is included!"

"Mama, Grandma wasn't the first person I heard say that Whisper was my father," Lay stammered. "Is it true?" Lay looked at her mother perplexed by what she'd just heard. She'd had a crush on Whisper ever since she could remember. He was the one person that she measured men against. She even came on to him and tried to kiss him not too long ago. "Tell me the truth Ma, 'cause I came on to Whisper one time, and—"

"What?" Big Lee snapped in a panic. "What did you do?"

"I tried to kiss him," Lay replied sorrowfully. "It was the night I stabbed Byrd, and I was at the lounge, drunk. Whisper walked me home and tucked me in on the couch. He was being supportive like the good godfather he is, and I tried to kiss him in one absent-minded moment."

"Did he kiss you back?" Mrs. Wilson huffed. Both Big Lee and

Lay shot their eyes over at her.

"No, ma'am! As a matter of fact, Whisper instantly pushed me away and asked what I was doing. He was mortified and set me straight!" Lay confessed. "That explains it! He knew I wasn't aware that he's my father. That's why Whisper wouldn't kiss me because he's my father!"

"What the fuck is going on?" Whisper seethed, feeling confused. "Did you just say that I'm your father?" Everyone turned around and stared at Whisper, who was in shock.

"Whisper, calm down," Big Lee cooed. "I can explain everything!"

"Well damn, Mama! Whisper didn't know either?" Lay scoffed. "What's that about?" Big Lee turned to face Lay with a discombobulated look on her face. "Why did you keep this from us? I mean, I always thought I looked like him and his mama, but I didn't think nothing of it because you said Cecil was my father!"

"Ann, why didn't you tell me the truth?" Whisper added. "I deserved to know the truth! I would have married you if I would have known you were carrying my baby!"

"Whisper, you weren't interested in being no husband or no father! You were out there banging and got caught up. I came to see you while you were in prison, and you weren't interested in pursuing a relationship with me." Big Lee sobbed. "You told me that I should move on with my life because you didn't know how much time you were facing. I was about to tell you that I was pregnant with your baby, and to hear those words broke my heart!"

"Fuck that, Ann! You should have told me, and maybe it would have put things in a different perspective!" Whisper snapped. "If you would have just told me, Ann! I would have probably changed my ways! Plus, when I got locked up, you were messing around with Cecil, and I thought y'all was together."

"How could you be so blind and stupid?" Big Lee whimpered. "You were the one with me every night, not Cecil. Just because we were always together during the day didn't mean we were together at night! Duh, Whisper! Nigga, stop playing dumb! You knew what it did, what it do, and what we'd done!"

"So why did you marry that nigga Cecil if you knew you were carrying my baby?" Whisper asked angrily. Big Lee looked over at her mother and stared at Mrs. Wilson vehemently.

"It was my mama's bright idea," Big Lee uttered. "She thought that it looked bad to her church friends for her daughter to be seventeen and pregnant. Her peers just make their kids get abortions and pretend like their daughters had miscarriages, but not Sister Wilson's daughter. She was going to have her baby, and then be pressured into marrying her best friend's son later down the line, because that's who she assumed was Lay's father. You were in jail, so I just went along with the shit. I was young and dumb, and petrified of my mama! Mama didn't know that Layloni was your baby, and she assumed that Cecil had to be because he was the one she always saw me with every day, and again, she and Cecil's mother were good friends." Big Lee looked over at Whisper sincerely. "I should have told you, Whisper. I should have told you a long time ago, but I just didn't know how to clear this mess up." Big Lee hunched her shoulders and stepped forward. "Aaaahhhh!" Big Lee had stepped into the broken glass that was lying on the floor. It went through her sock and cut her foot.

"Mama, why didn't you have on some house shoes?" Lay fussed. "You always getting on me about walking around barefoot!"

"I know, baby girl. I've just been under a lot of stress lately," Big Lee complained. Whisper came over and helped Big Lee over to a stool to sit down. Next, he left to go get the first aid kit out of the bathroom to fix up her foot.

"You're under a lot of stress because you've been carrying around all those lies and deceptions! Lee Ann, I don't know who taught you to be a liar, but you should have known better!" Big Lee looked at her mother in disbelief.

"You want to talk about liars, Mother?" Big Lee seethed. "I learned how to lie from the best, because you're the master of deception! Let's talk about how Cam and Ax are really the pastor's children!"

"Huh!" Lay shouted in disbelief. "Who is Pastor?" Mrs. Wilson looked over at Lay with a panicked look on her face. Whisper walked past Mrs. Wilson and looked back at her with a smirk on his face. Big Lee had told him about this last night after she'd had a conversation with her father. It had been a secret between Mr. and Mrs. Wilson, but he wanted his daughter to know the truth.

"Shut your mouth, Lee Ann! You don't know what you're talking about." Mrs. Wilson grunted. "I don't know who told you those lies, but Cameron and Axel are your father's children! So don't you go shooting off your mouth to Deacon Sr. about your false truths!" Big Lee laughed as Whisper cleaned the cut on her foot.

"You can cut your act, good sister," Big Lee insisted and laughed.

"And your little secret won't leave this room, but just know that my father told me everything last night. He was in a sharing mood, and you know how he gets when he's in a sharing mood, Mother."

"Don't you go shaming Deacon Sr.'s name with your lies, Lee Ann!" shouted Mrs. Wilson angrily. Big Lee laughed at her mother because Mrs. Wilson was determined to take that lie to the grave.

"Daddy used to get mad at Mama all the time because she used to spend so much time at the church. They'd argue for hours, then Daddy would get pissed and go down to the Gateway Lounge to get drunk. You know he's the reason why I bought the lounge in the first place. I said this would be a place where my daddy could come and have a piece of mind. That's why I had that apartment done so that he could have a place to crash when he didn't feel like going home to the good sister. That's why she ran to California, and I was happy to pay for their relocation!" Big Lee hissed smugly.

"Shut up, Lee Ann!" Mrs. Wilson shouted.

"No, Mama! I'm not going to shut up," Big Lee countered. "I'm going to tell all of your business to my daughter, and I'm going to come clean and tell my daughter the truth about everything." Big Lee grabbed a cigarette off the counter and fired it up. "Now, my mama had a long-standing affair with Pastor Mitchell. His wife was dying of cancer and, at first, Mama was helping her out with hospice because it was the Christian thing to do, but that tide turned when she became deathly ill. Pastor Mitchell baptized his penis inside of my mama's wading waters at his time of sorrows, and Cameron was produced. She's a married woman, so it wouldn't matter if she had a son, but two years later, Axel came, who just so happened to be named after Pastor Mitchell's great, great, great, great grandfather. Daddy said you had the name picked out before he could even make a suggestion." Mrs. Wilson glared at Big Lee angrily.

"Look at you… you smug, fat bitch! Do you think you actually did something by revealing my dirty laundry to Lay? You're just like me, daughter, so you ain't no better! Your father loved those boys as if they were his own, and he forgave me for it! He understood that I was weak, and at the time, he just couldn't give me what I needed." A single tear cascaded down Mrs. Wilson's cheek as she bared her soul to them. "But your father wasn't a saint either! He had women all over the neighborhood that he was fucking on the regular! I wouldn't be surprised if y'all don't have other siblings around this motherfucker that you don't know about!"

"Aaaahhh! Grandma cursed!" Lay giggled. Everyone looked over at her with frowns on their faces. "Sorry," she apologized in a small voice. Big Lee continued to look at her daughter for a second then smiled. Suddenly, she broke out in laughter and couldn't stop herself.

"What's wrong with her?" Mrs. Wilson scoffed.

"Ain't nothing wrong with me," Big Lee assured her and continued to laugh. "I am my mother's child, and that's a fact!" Everyone looked at her dumbfounded as she continued to bust a gut. It felt good to come clean to Lay and Whisper about the paternity. Now it was time for them to become a real family and put all this secrecy behind them.

CHAPTER FIVE

"*G*ood morning, sleepy head," Angie whispered softly into Ax's ear.

"Good morning, beautiful," Ax moaned. She rolled off the side of him as he turned over on his back. Angie climbed on top of him and planted a kiss on his lips. "About last night, huh?"

"Yeah, it was pretty wild." Angie giggled. "You're a beast, Axel Wilson!"

"That's what the ladies tell me," he bragged. "But I'm not interested in other ladies. I'm more interested in getting to know you, Amanda." Angie smiled as she leaned down and kissed his lips again.

"What do you want to know?" she asked coyly. "I've been taking care of myself ever since I was thirteen years old. My big brother's in jail because he's a stupid muthafucka, and even in there, he's still dumb as hell!"

"Oh yeah? What's your brother's name? I might know him," Ax offered. Angie looked at him hesitantly.

"I doubt if you know my brother," Angie quickly replied. "We're from Columbia, Missouri."

"Oh yeah! Where about? My brothers Rico and Ralph went to

Mizzou for about three years before they decided to drop out. We used to go up there with them all the time to conduct business with a few white boys they knew from around there. They grow the best skunk weed around the state. We use it to make edibles to sell," Ax explained. "I'll have to bring you some."

"I'd like that. I've tried edibles a few times, and I felt amazing," she said cheerfully.

"And I like you." Ax smiled back. His phone started to vibrate in his pants. "Who the fuck could that be?"

"Don't answer it," Angie suggested. Ax looked at her strangely.

"I always have to answer my phone. It could be my sister, one of my brothers, or my niece, Lay."

"You guys are close, aren't you?" Angie probed curiously.

"Yes we are, and after my brother's death, my sister has really become overprotective," Ax explained. "I spent the first week over her house, because I couldn't stand being at home alone. The next week, I was at my niece's house, because she and her bestie were having a hard time. My niece Layloni didn't sleep a wink for the first two weeks. That's why I stayed close to them to make sure they were okay. Now all she does is sleep, but I have a feeling that she's coming around. I saw her with her dude, and I know he'll make sure my niece is A1."

"You really love your nieces," Angie uttered.

"Damn right!" Ax replied.

"But I notice you talk about Layloni differently. You favor her more over the other one; why is that?" Angie wondered. Ax sat up in the bed and propped himself up with pillows on the headboard.

"Hand me a cigarette," Ax uttered, pointing off to the distance. Angie got up to get a cigarette and a lighter off the dresser. "Layloni is Ann's biological daughter. Ew Baby is Lay's best friend, and my sister took her in so that she wouldn't go to foster care."

"That explains why she doesn't look like any of you," Angie pointed out then smirked. "I noticed that the two of you hang out a lot more than you and Layloni. Every time I was at the gambling house, the two of you were there… together." Ax hit his cigarette and studied Angie.

"Ew Baby is my rider," Ax offered. "And no, I'm not fucking her. She's my niece's best friend, and that's bad for business."

"See, that's what I was looking for," said Angie intrigued.

"What?" Ax asked with a confused look on his face.

"The way you answered the question lets me know that you're suspect," Angie replied and laughed. "And before you ask another dumb question, let me explain. You didn't say that she's like a niece to you. You said she was your niece's best friend; there's a difference you know."

"How is there a difference?" Ax uttered. "I don't fuck around with my niece's friends. Besides, Ew Baby is really my sister's husband's daughter, so Lay and Ew Baby are actually sisters."

"Really? I didn't know Ce…" Angie caught herself. She almost told Ax that Cecil didn't tell her that piece of information.

"You didn't know what?" Ax asked coyly.

"I didn't know that your sister was so sneaky. She doesn't seem like the type. Does the girls know the truth?" Angie pried.

"Naw, they don't know. There's a lot that none of us know about Ann's life, and only my sister knows the truth." Ax pondered. His phone went off again. "Hand me my pants so I can answer my phone." Angie leaned down and grabbed Ax's phone out of his pocket. A few blue capsules fell out of his pocket, and Angie stared at them for a few seconds. She lifted up and stared at Ax strangely, because he didn't seem like a drug addict. *Maybe that's from one of the packs he's selling, but Ax doesn't nickel and dime petty hustle,* Angie thought. "What's the matter with you?" asked Ax, frowning.

"What's this?" asked Angie, holding up one of the pills. Ax looked at it then at her.

"What does it look like?" he asked. He snatched it out of her hand and opened it up. He knocked some of the powder on top of his hand then snorted it off with his right nostril. He put the rest of it on his hand and snorted it into the other nostril.

"Aye! I ain't trying to get mixed up with no dope fiend," Angie stammered.

"Good, 'cause I ain't no dope fiend. I just like to party hard sometimes, and a little cocaine ain't gon' hurt nobody," Ax joked. He grabbed Angie by the arm and pulled her to him. "But if you want to end this…" His dick rose up and poked her on the arm. "You can end this right now." Angie stared at Ax's wild gaze. He looked like he was smitten already, and Angie could use his addiction as a way to make him fall in love with her.

"Naw, ain't nothing wrong with it as long as I know about it," she replied. "I bump a lil' sometimes."

"Well we're going to get along just fine, darling!" Ax sang and smiled. He planted a passionate kiss against Angie's lips. He was ready for round three, and Angie was up for the challenge. This explained his stamina and sex drive, but the come down is what she was worried about. Would he be irritable and flip out like an old boyfriend used to do? However, heroin and cocaine are two different drugs, and Ax seemed like he could handle it; at least she hoped he could.

****

Lay had been texting back and forth with Byrd for the past few days. She hadn't talked to him all day, and every time she called him, his phone went to voicemail. This distracted her from paying attention in class, besides the fact she found out this morning that Cecil wasn't her father. Her thoughts were scattered all over the place as she stared out of the window. The professor was surprised by the lack of participation from Lay, and he even presented a question to her to pull her into the discussion. She was flustered that he called her out in front of the class and took offense to his actions.

"Professor Miller, I didn't raise my hand. Why did you call on me?" Lay asked defensively.

"Because, this is my class, Ms. Wilson, and I can call on anyone if I choose to do so," Professor Miller replied. His timer went off, warning him that he had three minutes before class ended. "Can I see you after class, Layloni?" She looked at him smugly because she didn't want to talk to him. *All he needs to do is go over the reading assignment and dismiss the class*, she thought. "Don't forget to finish up the chapter, and be prepared for the quiz on Thursday. Class dismissed."

Everyone shuffled out of their seats and exited the classroom. Lay looked around and watched as her fellow classmates looked at her sympathetically. Professor Miller seemed to be targeting Lay, and no one ever wanted to stay afterwards to talk with him. He was one of the hardest professors at the university, and if you passed his class with a B average, you were lucky. Lay got up out of her seat and walked toward his desk. She wanted this meeting to be over ASAP, because she wanted to find Byrd.

"What's up, Professor Miller?" Lay asked, walking toward his desk.

"Ms. Wilson, you have missed several of my classes, and your grade has fallen a letter. You're usually very forthcoming with the class discussions, yet you have fallen silent. May I ask what happened?" Lay looked at him smugly.

"Life happened," she replied sarcastically. "Didn't the registrar's office inform you that my uncle was violently killed?" Professor Miller looked at her quite concerned.

"You have my condolences, Ms. Wilson, and that explains so much," he replied solemnly. "When I didn't see you in class for two weeks straight, I was concerned. I sent you an email. Did you receive it?"

"Yes, I received it, but I was a bit out of it. I saw my uncle's bullet-riddled body lying out on the floor, and it seriously affected me psychologically. I wasn't able to sleep for weeks because every time

I closed my eyes, I saw his lifeless body covered in blood." Professor Miller frowned as he watched Lay's face go into a depressive stare. "I tried to turn in my assignments, and I even did the extra credit questions. I know I'm not working up to my full potential, but my uncle's death was a tough blow."

"I take it the two of you were very close," Professor Miller speculated.

"Very," Lay replied. "He was more like a big brother than an uncle, and my mother always referred to him as her oldest."

"Again, I'm sorry, Layloni, and if there's anything I can do to help you, please don't hesitate to call me. I have no problems giving you an extension if you need it, but beware that your final paper is due soon. You need a passing grade from my class in order to graduate."

"I know, Professor Miller, and I promise I won't disappoint you," Lay assured him. "I started the prep work a while ago, and I feel confident that I will be finished on time."

"That's good to hear," he replied enthusiastically. "You're one of my star students, and I would hate to see all of your hard work go down the drain."

"Thanks, Professor, for your concern, but I got this!"

***

Lay pulled up to the house and parked her car in front of it. She tried to get in contact with Byrd on the ride home, but he still wasn't answering his phone. This aggravated her because she needed to talk to him about what she'd found out earlier from her mother. She couldn't believe that Whisper was her father and her mother never said anything to her about it. What else was Big Lee hiding from her, and why did she say that she was going to tell Lay the truth about everything? Lay was confused about so much and wanted to go climb in her bed to go to sleep, but she had to go to the lounge to work, and hopefully, she'd have time to talk with her mother.

****

Big Lee walked through the door and looked around the lounge as she made her way over to the bar. It had been three weeks since she'd gone into the lounge, and it felt strange to her once she came inside. Everyone had been looking for her to give their condolences about Cam, but she just didn't want to be bothered and stayed away.

"Hey, Mama," said Lay, smiling as she continued to work.

"Hey, baby." Big Lee sighed, sitting down on her stool. "Crazy morning, huh?"

Lay looked up at her mother uncomfortably.

"Yeah… it was definitely interesting," Lay uttered. "Mama, let me ask you a question. Why did you keep this a secret for so long?" Big Lee pulled out her cigarettes and fired one up.

"Because your mama's stupid, that's why! I've learned in my life that we let our pride and ego take over sometimes. Throw in being young, dumb, and full of cum, and you have an average teenager. I was afraid of being pregnant and alone, and I was scared. Oh Lay, I was scared. Whisper was deep off into the gang life, and every day was another day for him to gamble with his life. Whisper could throw his hands, and everyone knew he was a beast, so that made him a target. Niggas were scared of him, and it resulted in niggas starting that pistol play against him." Lay placed a double shot of Don Julio in front of her mother, along with a glass of water. Big Lee took a hit of her cigarette and stared out of the front window. "I remember when Whisper did his first murder. He was a wreck! Some niggas from over the way had shot at them one day when they were up at the park. Craig and Deacon had come up on some guns, and they decided that they were going to go get 'em. The usual suspects climbed into the old deuce and a quarter that Craig had saved up to buy, and they went searching."

"Mama, Uncle Craig had a deuce and a quarter?" Lay giggled. A smile came across Big Lee's face.

"Yes, child! And we used to go everywhere in that car," Big Lee reminisced.

"So, what happened?" Lay asked inquisitively. She loved to hear her mother tell stories about back in the day. It was like her family's history, and she wanted to know everything about it, especially since it's about her real father.

"Anyway, they parked about a block away and got out of the car. For some reason, they thought they asses was like a military force you see on television. Rico, Ralph, and Whisper used to sit up and watch action and karate movies all of the damn time." Big Lee reminisced and laughed. She took a drink of her water and put her cigarette out. "So they crept down the block and spotted some niggas standing out. It was a vacant lot that sat on the corner, and they hid on the side of it by an unoccupied building. Rico and Ralph started arguing about how they were going to attack, while Whisper stood listening and scoping out the scene. They all had smoked a dipped cigarette before they left the house, so all of them were wacked out of their minds. Craig got tired of hearing them argue, and Deacon was trying to stop them—"

"Their asses are always arguing at the wrong time," Lay interrupted and laughed.

"Don't they, though," Big Lee agreed and laughed. "Craig said Whisper must have gotten tired of waiting, because he said this nigga had come around the corner and just start shooting at the niggas. Everyone took off running, and Whisper started chasing them. My brothers came behind him and started running to catch up with Whisper, who was halfway up the street. Your daddy..." Big Lee paused for a moment and looked up at Lay, sorrowful. "I apologize for not telling you sooner. I should have been honest with you, Layloni, and I'm truly sorry." Lay lowered her gaze and twiddled with her fingers.

"Honestly, Mama, a part of me feels like I should be mad at you, but I'm not. Even though you hid the fact that Whisper is my father, he was still a major part of my life and played that role. He treated me like I was his daughter, and he always had my back. I can't say the same for Cecil, because I was too young to remember him."

"You didn't like him as a child. You used to cry every time he came near you," said Big Lee, and she laughed. "But when Whisper came home from jail, you were about two years old. He came out of his grandma's house and saw us sitting on the porch. He came down the street and stopped in front of the gate. I carried you down the steps to meet him, and you jumped right into his arms without me saying a word." Big Lee grabbed Lay's hand and kissed the back of it. She stared sincerely into her baby girl's eyes, and a big smile came across Lay's beautiful face.

"So finish the story, Mama! I want to hear what happened," Lay insisted. A warm smile spread across Big Lee's face.

"Okay, so Whisper had chased a nigga down a gangway into the alley. He fired a few shots, and the dude fell to the ground. Whisper walked up on dude and stared at him vehemently. He told Whisper, 'fuck you, ole dookie ass nigga,' so Whisper shot him twice in the head."

"Damn!" Lay called out and frowned. "Where were you at?"

"I was at home, nervous as a muthafucka." Big Lee chuckled. "Those niggas didn't know nothing about killing a person, but after that night, they did, though! Whisper came into my room looking crazy and shit. He didn't want to have sex like the usual, so we went straight to bed. He must have been dreaming about what happened because he woke up in a cold sweat. I jumped up with him because it scared me half to death. He grabbed me and hugged me tightly, then started telling me about what happened. He laid in my arms for hours, and we just held each other tightly. Next thing I know, something came over his ass, and he climbed on top of me and we—"

"Okay, Mama! I don't have to hear the rest of this," Lay interrupted, walking to the other end of the bar. Big Lee laughed, because she knew her daughter hated to hear her talk about sex, especially with Whisper. Lay waited on a customer then came back over to her mother.

"What I was about to tell you, Lay, before you walked off," Big Lee scoffed. "That was the day you were conceived." Lay looked at her mother sideways.

"I was made as a result of a murder?" Lay mocked then frowned.

45

She pondered it for a moment while Big Lee knocked down her shot. She looked at her mother with a smirk on her face. "That's kind of dope as I think about it," Lay added. Big Lee looked at her skeptically for a second.

"Now that you mention it, baby girl, that is gangsta!" Big Lee gloated. "That's why your ass is crazy!"

"Correction, Mama. Y'all DNA is the reason why I'm crazy." Both women laughed in agreement, because Lay acted like both of her parents to the highest degree. She had more of Big Lee's attitude, but she'd get gutta with a muthafucka if that's what had to be done.

CHAPTER SIX

*B*ig Lee let the girls off early because they'd been working hard all week. It was a Tuesday night, and they were fully aware that somebody's Two Dollar Tuesday was poppin' off. Ew Baby had gotten a call from an acquaintance that ManMan was at The Imperial Palace. They had an interesting encounter the other day, and Ew Baby wanted to know if she was just tripping. She was at the gambling house with Ax, when he came up on her and complimented her outfit. They shared a little small talk then he walked away, but not before he smiled enthusiastically at her.

She had always had a crush on ManMan, ever since her freshman year of high school. Ew Baby was known to be a dirty girl because her mama was on dope, and she dressed like a bum. Lay was her best friend, and didn't like people teasing Ew Baby, so she begged her mama to take Ew Baby shopping, and Big Lee was happy to do it. After that, Big Lee got into the habit of buying Ew Baby clothes whenever they went shopping. She knew how much it bothered Lay to have her friend being teased and talked about, so she made sure that Ew Baby stayed on point.

"Are you ready?" asked Lay, standing in Ew Baby's doorway.

"Yeah, I'm ready," Ew Baby replied, checking herself out in the dressing mirror.

"Ooouuuiiii, Ew Baby! You're wearing that dress!" Lay declared. "Who you trying to catch toniggggght?" Ew Baby had on a red cotton long-sleeve dress with a deep V coming down the front and the back of it. She put on a black blazer and paired it with a pair of black patent leather red bottoms. She only needed the jacket to walk into the club, because she would be shedding it as soon as they hit the door. "And those heels are giving me life!" Lay declared.

"I know, right." Ew Baby gloated, rubbing her hands down the side of her thighs. "You ain't short stopping yourself, hot mama!" Lay had on a blue two-piece skirt set with the cropped shirt that fit tightly under her breasts, and a three-quarter length pencil skirt that stopped in the middle of her calves. She added a long black mink vest and finished it off with a pair of blue red bottom stilettos.

"Why thank you, darling," Lay replied. "I'm feeling myself tonight."

"And that Chinese bob with the part down the middle that I whipped up on you is clowning!" Ew Baby bragged.

"Ain't it tho'! Thanks, sis," Lay signified and shook her hair. "We should get going because you know parking is going to be a bitch... And that line!"

"We ain't got to worry about that line," Ew Baby scoffed. "I got the hook up at the door."

"That's music to my ears!" Lay sang. "Let's get it!"

Ew Baby wasn't lying when she said she had the hook up at The

Imperial Palace. It was a line down the street, and the two women just walked up to the front of it and went inside without paying. Ew Baby knew a lot of people, especially men, because she'd been hanging out with Ax. If Ew Baby told Lay about some of the stuff Ax had her involved in, she would be furious with her!

The ladies walked up to the bar and looked around as they waited for the bartender to serve them. Ew Baby spotted one of ManMan's boys, so she knew he wasn't too far away. Lay ordered them shots, and they knocked those down quickly. They'd already taken a few at the house while they were getting dressed and smoked a blunt of that high-powered gas on the ride over to the club.

"It's litty in here!" Ew Baby shouted, dancing to the music.

"Ain't it though!" Lay agreed. She picked up her second shot and knocked it down like a pro. "Woooo! I'm ready to get it in!"

"Come on, gurlll... Let's go," said Ew Baby, pulling Lay away from the bar. The ladies went and posted up at a high table over against the wall. They danced to the music and talked to random people they knew who walked past them. Lay and Ew Baby were like street royalty, and people were always trying to be down with them. Everyone who was anyone in St. Louis knew about the Wilson family. Big Lee was the queen of the city, and her daughter was a prime choice. All the hot niggas loved to try to get at Lay, but she wasn't interested. She had a table full of drinks, and a bottle of Moet that a nigga had sent her, sitting on the table. She thanked all of them for their generosity, but she let them down easy. She wasn't interested in no average ass street hustler, and all of them were nickel and dime ass niggas, who were probably trying to latch on to get a bone to come up off of. Needless to say, they were wasting their time.

Byrd was sitting on the other side of the club with his boys. He had finally texted Lay's phone back from earlier, but she didn't respond to his message. Byrd was moving around trying to make sure his money was straight, so he didn't have time to text or call Lay. Ever since Cam gave him his blessing, Byrd was trying to get rid of all of it, because he didn't want to get caught up. Red walked up to the table and sat down with his drinks. He looked back and smiled as he took a beer out of the bucket.

"Damn! I just saw Lay, and she was lookin' right!" Red called out.

"Oh yeah," said ManMan, lustfully rubbing his hands together. "What do she have on?" Byrd glared at the two men and took a sip of his beer. "I bet it's something tight and sexy!"

"Yeah, it's tight, and it's definitely sexy!" Red gawked. "Boy, what I wouldn't do to have a taste of that sweet pussy."

"You ain't got no chances with that," Byrd scoffed. Red looked at him smugly.

"What you mean?" Red snapped. Byrd looked at him with a smirk on his face.

"Take it how you want to, Red," he replied nonchalantly. "But you know it's true."

"Nigga! You know Lay don't want your ass!" ManMan teased and laughed. "We all know that I'm the only nigga sitting here that's got a chance with her!"

"Nigga, get the fuck out of here!" Byrd called out and laughed. "She don't want your ass either!" They all fell out laughing at ManMan.

"We gon' see," said ManMan, getting up from the table.

"What you finna do?" Red asked, getting up from the table too.

"Just sit back and watch a master at work," ManMan ordered. An arrogant smile came across his face because he was about to make Lay take notice of him. "The night is young, and I've got work to do to hook that big fish!"

****

Lay and Ew Baby were kicking it with a few females that they knew from the hood. The niggas were crowding them, and the women were swatting them away like flies. The drinks had been flowing, and the ladies were feeling quite tipsy. The music was lit, and the ladies were showing off their moves for all to see. Byrd was standing off to the side with his homeboys, and they were a captive audience at the Lay and Ew Baby show. ManMan walked up to Byrd and smiled a devilish grin at him. It was time for him to make his move, and he wanted his biggest hater to be front and center.

"Sit back and watch the master at work," ManMan bragged. He put his arm on Byrd's shoulder and smirked.

"What the fuck you talking about?" Byrd scoffed, annoyed. ManMan smiled a shit-eating grin at him.

"Just watch!" ManMan replied, sipping his beer. A waitress walked over to Lay's table with a bucket of Moet being lit up by sparkles, and two champagne glasses. She whispered something to Lay in her ear and pointed in ManMan's direction. ManMan held up his beer, and Lay looked at him and smiled. She nodded her head at him in acknowledgement, and then pulled the bottle out of the bucket. She popped the cork, and the ladies cheered as Nicki Minaj and Gotti's song "Rake It Up" came beating through the club. Lay looked over at Byrd seductively and licked her lips, biting the bottom one. "Ewww, Byrd, man! Did you see that?" ManMan moaned in excitement. "She wants me!" Byrd smirked as Lay walked toward them with two glasses of champagne. They both watched Lay closely as she made her way up to where they were standing.

"Thanks for the champagne," said Lay, handing ManMan one of the glasses.

"You're welcome, Layloni," ManMan replied with a big smile on his face. "You looking mighty sexy in that outfit." Lay looked herself over then back up at ManMan.

"Thanks," she replied and smirked, then glanced over at Byrd.

"I'm surprised to see you out tonight, because normally you're at the Gateway working," ManMan mentioned.

"Well, my mama felt that I needed a night out, so she let me and Ew Baby off to have some fun," Lay explained. She turned and walked over to Byrd and handed him the other glass of champagne. Next, she whispered in his ear because she didn't want ManMan to hear what she had to say. "You know I don't like being ignored," Lay whispered. "You know you have to be punished for ignoring me today. Did you miss me?"

"You know I did," Byrd uttered, looking her up and down. ManMan was dumbfounded at the way Lay was giving her attention to

Byrd, and he was the one who bought her a bottle of champagne. "Did you miss me?"

"Yes, baby," Lay moaned seductively. A bigger smile came across Byrd's face. He and Lay stared intensely into each other's eyes because their magnetic attraction was generating all kinds of sexual energy.

"Well show me," he demanded sternly.

He continued to watch her intently, as he stared into Lay's eyes suggestively. He saw how her intoxication was starting to take over, but Lay returned the intense gaze with Byrd then smiled at him devilishly. She cupped her hand behind his head and started grinding her pelvis against him. They continued to stare into each other's eyes as she groped all over him. She turned and pushed her ass against his crotch and started bouncing it up against him. She leaned to the side and looked back up at him with a serious expression and bit her bottom lip seductively. He was enjoying her display of affection and put his hand on her hip to hold on. He looked over at ManMan and took a drink of his champagne while he enjoyed his dance. ManMan stared in disbelief as Lay continued to freak Byrd down. Byrd's serious facial expression never changed as he watched his baby work. The way he was studying her almost seemed like he was impartial to what was going on. You couldn't tell if he was enjoying it or not, because his brow was furrowed with a stern look on his face.

The song had ended, and by that time, ManMan was too fit to be tied. He felt like he should have been the one getting the lap dance instead of Byrd; the one who didn't buy Lay shit!

Lay stood up and started rocking her hips back and forth in front of Byrd, while his hand continued to hold onto her hip. She turned and smiled at him coyly, then planted her lips firmly against his. She cupped the back of his head and tilted hers slightly as she slid her tongue into his mouth. Byrd closed his eyes and savored this moment, because Lay was letting all these niggas know that he was the one she had chosen. He tried to tell ManMan's ass at the burial that Lay was his chick, but sometimes niggas didn't want to listen, so you had to show them better than you could tell them.

"What the fuck is going on!" ManMan shouted in outrage.

"That's what I want to know," Red gawked. "This nigga's been holding out on us all of this time." Lay pulled away from Byrd and kissed him quickly once more. Then she wiped her lip-gloss off his lips and smiled at him warmly as she did it.

"Am I going home with you tonight?" Lay questioned. Byrd smirked at his baby because she was showing out.

"What you think?" he asked, frowning. "I'll be over there to get you in a few minutes. Go finish entertaining your fans." Lay looked at Byrd coyly, then turned to walk away. He smacked her on the ass, and Lay stopped to look at him with a smirk on her face.

"Ewww, baby! You know I like that shit!" Lay whined and giggled. She held her ass out at him, and he smacked it again. "Yeah… like that!" Lay turned and kissed Byrd once more then walked off doing her best strut. Her hips swayed to the music, and her ass bounced to the beat while she made her way back over to her table. Byrd's dick was rock hard and his ego super inflated, because damn near every nigga up in the club was staring at him in disbelief.

"What the fuck, Byrd Man!" Red shouted. "You smashing that?" Byrd looked over at his envious friends, held up his glass of champagne, and took a sip in victory. He didn't feel like a response was necessary, because Lay made sure that everyone knew that Byrd was her man.

CHAPTER SEVEN

"*N*igga, what the fuck was that?" ManMan spat enviously as he washed his hands in the men's room sink. "I mean… you've been smashing Layloni, and you didn't care to mention it to me!"

"She ain't want nobody to know, so I respected her wishes," Byrd replied nonchalantly. "Besides, I tried to tell you at Cam's burial, but you didn't want to listen. Plus, it wasn't any of your business." Byrd looked over at Lay through the crack in the door and smiled.

"Wait a minute! It's none of my business?" ManMan snapped, frustrated. "I'm your best friend, and I feel like that was some best friend shit! I tell you everything, Byrd." Byrd looked over at ManMan unapologetically.

"Look, dude. I didn't tell you, so get over it." Byrd shrugged. "I kept telling you that she wasn't into light-skinned niggas, but you refused to listen to me." ManMan cut his eyes at his best friend since elementary school, because he continuously let him look stupid in front of Lay. They walked out of the bathroom and went back over to their table.

"Whatever, nigga," ManMan scoffed as they strolled across the club. "That was some dirty shit, dude! You let me constantly make a fool out of myself on the daily, I might add."

"Again, it wasn't any of your business. Just look at it this way…" Byrd set his glass down on the table. "You know now." He walked off, and ManMan watched as he went over to Lay. He whispered something in her ear, and a smile spread across her face. Byrd grabbed Lay's hand and led her off somewhere. ManMan watched in an envious rage, because he wanted to be the one fucking with Layloni Wilson.

Byrd took Lay out to his car in the parking lot. He wanted to talk with her privately for a moment, because he missed her and hadn't talked to his bae all day. Lay was feeling awesome, and she hoped that Byrd was taking her to smoke a blunt, because a little grass would be on point right about now.

"I hope you're taking me to go smoke a blunt," Lay professed with a hint of an attitude.

"Girl, be quiet and come on!" Byrd huffed. "You always talking shit." Lay laughed as she ran up on him. She wrapped her arms around his waist and giggled as they made it to his car. He opened the passenger side door and held it open for her. "Come on and get in, Lay." She let him go and stepped backward.

"Do I know you, mister?" Lay teased. "My mama told me not to get in strange cars with strange men." Byrd licked his lips and smiled.

"I got some candy for you," he offered, grabbing his crotch. Lay made an 'o' with her mouth and put her hand up to it.

"Oooohhh… you got candy for me?" she asked playfully and giggled. "What kind is it because I only like dark chocolate?"

"I know… with nuts!" He grinned. "Come here, baby. I miss the fuck out of you!" Lay walked over to her man and wrapped her arms around his waist. She hugged him tightly because she missed him too.

"Ain't that, that nigga Byrd over there?" huffed Booker, one of Byrd's known enemies.

"Yeah, that's that nigga," said Dump, Shakey's big brother. "I see he's with that bitch Lay. You know she beat up my little sister over that nigga!"

"I heard," Booker acknowledged. "She's too cute to be with that nigga. Why she fuckin' with him?"

"I don't know, but I don't like that nigga," Dump insisted with a scowl on his face. "He was fucking with my sister and didn't even want to give a nigga a play. I should rob his bitch ass!"

"We can do that, bro, but we need to do some planning," Booker suggested. "But for right now, we can go say hello to that nigga!"

Byrd saw Booker walking toward them with Dump following closely behind. He noticed Dump looking over his shoulder, so he figured they must be up to something. Lay peeped the same thing and sat down in the seat. She knew Byrd kept a burner up under both seats, so she quickly reached under it and grabbed the Glock.

"Baby, I think we should get back to the club," said Lay, giggling. She leaned over and grabbed the other hammer from up under the driver's seat, while Byrd watched her closely.

"It's all good, baby," Byrd replied. Lay stood up and hugged Byrd tightly. She slid one of the burners into his hand, and he looked down into her eyes.

"It's whatever, Byrd," Lay whispered, and she put her arm around his waist.

"What's up, Byrd," Booker spat with a frown on his face.

"Ain't shit up," Byrd replied nonchalantly. Lay glared at both of the men disapprovingly.

"What's up, Lay?" said Booker, staring at her lustfully. "What you doin' out here with this bitch ass nigga?"

"The only bitch ass nigga I see is—"

"What you want, Booker?" Byrd interrupted. "And Dump… since when have you been hanging out with this nigga?"

"Booker's been my boy," Dump replied defensively. "Where's Shakey?" Lay started laughing.

"Somewhere," Byrd replied sarcastically. "Look, neither one of you don't want no smoke, so why don't y'all go play with each other or something!" Booker looked at Byrd vehemently.

"You real tough standing out here by yourself," Dump hissed.

"What makes you think he's by himself?" ManMan spat with Ew Baby standing next to him. She had Lay's purse in her hand, but Lay knew Ew Baby had her blade ready to go. "Why don't y'all niggas go play with y'all self like my homie said?" Booker turned around and saw ManMan, Ew Baby, Red, and a few more of their crew standing behind him.

"I guess you saw the bat signal," Booker joked with a sarcastic grin across his face.

"Naw, nigga," Byrd replied. "He spared your life."

"Please believe," Lay added. Booker looked at Lay and smiled.

"PYT, when you're ready to get with a real man, give me a call," Booker cooed and blew a kiss at her.

"I'm already with one, and it don't get no realer than the Byrd Man, bitch ass nigga!" Lay hissed. Booker let out a menacing laugh as he stared at the couple. He had plans for Lay's sweet little smart-ass mouth, and Byrd already knew what was up, so he had plans to catch Booker out in traffic.

"I'll see you," Booker assured Byrd, then turned and walked away. Byrd stared at the two men as they walked off the parking lot. He knew he'd better watch his back, because Booker liked to rob niggas, and now that he knew Lay was his girl, that had him marked for open season.

"Thanks, baby," said Byrd, looking down at Lay. He kissed her lips quickly and then her forehead.

"You're welcome, baby," Lay replied lovingly. "Just remember... I always got your back!"

****

The gang decided to go to The Courtesy Diner to eat breakfast. Byrd was feeling a bit uneasy, because Booker and Dump slid up on him and his baby. He couldn't be putting Lay in that type of danger, so they needed to be more careful in the future. ManMan rode with Ew Baby to the diner, and it was taking them a long time to pull up.

"Aye! How you know where to grab my burners?" Byrd asked, turning to face Lay.

"I'm always on point, Byrd. When you've been involved in as many robbery attempts as I have, you learn to peep your surroundings and the scene," Lay explained. "You must have forgotten that you told me when we first started messing around that you kept one under each seat. Remember that night we were out riding, and the police slid up on us?" Byrd looked at her skeptically for a second.

"You know what? I do remember that night," Byrd recalled. "You snuck out of the house, and it was your freshman year of college!"

"I was eighteen, but my mama still treated me like I was a kid," Lay added.

"That's the shit that parents do," Byrd conveyed to her. He looked and noticed that Lay had on the diamond B necklace that he'd given her the day they broke up. For some reason, he didn't remember seeing it on in the club, so he wondered where did it come from. "Aye, what's that around your neck?" Lay grabbed her B and swiveled it back and forth across the chain.

"What you talking about?" Lay asked in a teasing manner. "You talking about my B for my bae, boo, baby?" Byrd pulled Lay over toward him.

"You know I love you, right?" Byrd questioned. Lay saw the vulnerability in his eyes, and it made her feel a bit anxious. "Cam came to see me right before he died. He wanted to know what was going to happen with us since you stabbed me." Lay stared at Byrd, surprised. She asked Cam not to go see him, but obviously, in the true Wilson Family manner, he didn't listen.

"I asked Cam not to go see you." Lay sighed.

"It's all good," Byrd assured her. "Because what he said to me was real. It was my fault for getting mad at you, and I see what you were talking about once niggas saw that we were together."

"All the niggas want to get a taste of this juicy pop," Lay rapped. She snapped her fingers and shook her hair as she danced.

"Shut up!" Byrd insisted as he laughed. "You ugly!"

"So! You like it," Lay shot back. "Now lean over and give me some sugar."

"Nope! I ain't giving you shit!" Byrd shot back. Lay looked at him, amused. "You lean yo' ass over here and give me some suga!" Lay smiled and leaned her head over, and he grabbed the back of Lay's head. He licked his tongue out at her, and a smile came across her face. She licked her tongue out and touched the tip of his before she seized the entire thing in her mouth. She lifted up over the middle console and placed herself onto Byrd's lap. They were going hot and heavy in his car and didn't pay any attention to their surroundings.

"It's going to be easy to get this nigga," Booker declared into the phone. "And Lay gon' be the one to help us."

CHAPTER EIGHT

*B*ig Lee walked into her bedroom, and Whisper was fast asleep. They didn't get a chance to talk after her mother blurted out the truth about Lay. The look on his face when he left out of the house said volumes, because he didn't even bother to call to check on her like usual. Big Lee climbed in the bed and pulled the covers over her body. She turned so that her back was against his, and she let out a long, deep sigh as she settled into her spot.

"Since when have you slept with your back to me?" Whisper grumbled. He turned over on his other side and scooted his body closer to Big Lee's. "You acting funny, Ann?" Big Lee turned over to face Whisper and smiled at him.

"I thought you were sleep, and I didn't want to disturb you," she replied. Whisper leaned in and kissed her on the lips.

"I want you to explain to me why it was so difficult for you to tell me that Lay was my daughter," Whisper breathed.

"I don't know, Whisper." Big Lee sighed. "I really don't know. There were so many times throughout the years when I wanted to tell you the truth. I thought that you would hate me, but I guess I was just being dumb."

"I'm not gon' lie, Ann, I had to go think long and hard about this situation," Whisper admitted. "I went to have a long talk with Craig and Deacon."

"Why did you go talk to them?" Big Lee questioned.

"Because, they're my big brothers, too," Whisper replied arrogantly. "But for real, Ann, I had to wrap my head around this shit, because it makes me question what else you're hiding."

"I'm not hiding shit else, Whisper. I promise," Big Lee assured him. "And I'm going to tell Lay and Ew Baby the truth about Cecil being Ew Baby's daddy."

"How do you think Lay's going to react?"

"I don't know." Big Lee worried. "She was cool with finding out the truth about you. However, I don't know how she's going to feel about Cecil being Ew Baby's daddy."

"I think it's Ew Baby that you should worry about," Whisper warned. "She's the wild card."

"I agree, but I hope she doesn't get mad at me." Big Lee sighed. "I felt like they should have told her a long time ago, because I felt that it wasn't my place to do so. Cecil begged me not to say anything to her because he wanted us to do it together."

"Together! For what?" Whisper questioned. "That nigga's an ass!" Big Lee rubbed her leg against his thigh and brought it up his leg. Whisper moved his leg back away from her because she was trying to distract him by making his dick hard.

"Uhhh unnnn… Ann! You're on punishment," Whisper scoffed.

"I ain't giving you no dick for at least a week."

"At least a week!" she shouted in protest. "Don't you think that's a bit harsh?"

"Nope!" he protested sternly. "And if you keep talking, I might make it a month." Big Lee smiled as she turned over on her other side. "I'll take your punishment, but I bet you cave before I do." She pushed her ass into his semi erect rod and nestled the rest of her body against him as she prepared to go to sleep. She knew that Whisper had no problems holding out on her. She was the one that was always horny, and it was going to be a long week if his ass acted his normal stubborn self!

****

"We can pull over in the park," ManMan suggested, rubbing Ew Baby's leg.

"What the fuck do you take me for, ManMan?" Ew Baby scoffed. "I know I'm a hoe, but damn! I ain't that fucking easy! Besides, you were just all on Lay at the club, sending her bottles of champagne and shit!"

"That's because I didn't know that she was with Byrd," ManMan confessed. "If I would have known that, I would have been jumped on you, Ew Baby. I've been clocking you, even though it seemed like I wasn't." Ew Baby looked at ManMan with her lips turned up.

"Yeah, I've seen you watching me, but that doesn't excuse the fact that you were playing nice with me to get at Lay," Ew Baby complained. "I ain't no slouch you know."

"I know, Ew Baby, and I'm sorry," ManMan apologized. "And I've always said that you were cute! You can ask any of my boys."

"So if that's the case, why were you always on Lay?" Ew Baby questioned. ManMan had rolled a blunt in the process of them riding to the restaurant. He fired it up as he tried to sweet talk Ew Baby out of some pussy.

"Hell, Ew Baby! Who wouldn't try to get on Lay?" ManMan blurted out. "She's beautiful, smart, and—"

"The daughter of Big Lee," Ew Baby finished. "Niggas are always trying to get on her because of Mama. However, Lay ain't really into dudes like that because she doesn't trust them. She's seen men try to use Mama, so she'd rather be by herself and just deal with niggas when she wants to."

"So she's just using Byrd?" ManMan probed curiously, passing Ew Baby the blunt.

"I'm not saying that," Ew Baby answered in haste. "All I'm saying is that Lay don't seem like the relationship type. She deals with dudes for a while then she leaves them alone. That's all I'm saying."

"So are you the same way?" ManMan inquired. Ew Baby smiled at him and passed the blunt back.

"Naw, I'm a little different," Ew Baby replied. "I love being in a relationship because I like to focus on one person. Loyalty is difficult to find in this day and age, so I'm careful about who I fuck with. Plus, my uncles are always harassing anyone that I mess with, so it makes it difficult for dudes to even get close to me." Ew Baby paused for a second. "Damn! I forgot Cam is gone. I guess I only have one uncle to look out for me now."

"I ain't gon' lie, Ew Baby, I thought you and Ax had something going on," ManMan admitted. "You're always with him, and y'all look and act like a couple." Ew Baby laughed as she hit the blunt.

"That nigga would probably try to fight you if he heard you say that shit," Ew Baby mentioned and continued to laugh.

"Well don't tell him that I said that," ManMan replied and smirked. He leaned over and kissed Ew Baby on the neck while he slid his hand up under her dress.

"Nigga! What are you doing?" Ew Baby quaked.

"I'm just trying to see something," ManMan moaned. Ew Baby's eyes widened as she felt his fingers brush against her folds.

"I think you need to get back over in your seat," Ew Baby protested, throwing her elbow at him.

"I thought you were going to be with it, Ew Baby," ManMan whined. "So you're telling me that you don't want none of this dick?" Ew Baby stopped at the red light and turned to face ManMan with a frown on her face.

"I ain't say that, but you ain't got shit coming tonight! And again, you weren't stuttin' me earlier. You were all on Lay," Ew Baby emphasized.

"Well, at least let me suck your pussy," ManMan offered. One of Ew Baby's eyebrows went up as she looked curiously at him.

"I do love to get my pussy sucked," she admitted. "But I ain't fucking with you, ManMan! You got me fucked up tonight!" This angered ManMan, because at first Ew Baby would literally throw herself at him, but now she was acting brand new.

"You better pull this muthafucka over, Ew Baby!" ManMan shouted. "And let me suck that puuussy!" Ew Baby laughed at the way he said it and felt like what could it hurt. They were cutting through Forest Park as a shortcut to the restaurant. Ew Baby knew a spot over by the Muny Amphitheater that was deserted and secluded, so she turned and headed that way. "Damn! Where you going?"

"You'll see," she hissed. "You said you want to eat this puuussy, so I'm taking you somewhere where you can!" She hit a few more turns and pulled up in a dark area.

"Damn! I didn't even know about this place," said ManMan, intrigued.

"Don't be bringing your bitches to my spot," Ew Baby instructed then frowned.

"Shut up!" ManMan hissed, pushing Ew Baby on the arm. "Now, come here!" ManMan pulled Ew Baby toward him and stopped before their lips met. He stared into her eyes for a second then he kissed her passionately. Thoughts were running through Ew Baby's head because she did want ManMan, but she was still feeling some type of way about his obsession with Lay. Next, ManMan pulled Ew Baby over into his lap and slid his hand up her dress. Ew Baby broke away and breathed heavily while his fingers brushed against her folds. ManMan kissed the nape of her neck and licked down her cleavage, causing Ew Baby to almost cum on herself.

"I bet you're a freak," Ew Baby mentioned breathlessly.

"And some," ManMan moaned. He pushed Ew Baby face down

into the driver's seat and lifted the bottom of her dress up in one swoop. He pulled her G-string over to the side and slid his tongue up into her wet walls.

"Well damn!" Ew Baby moaned as ManMan slid his tongue inside of her. "That muthafucka feels like a dick!" ManMan chuckled as he continued to suck Ew Baby up. He moaned and groaned as he used his fingers and mouth to please Ew Baby. Her phone started ringing, and she realized that Lay and Byrd were waiting on them at the restaurant. "Ah damn, ManMan! We were supposed to be meeting Lay and Byrd at Courtesy Diner," she groaned. What he was doing to her felt too damn good, and she didn't want him to stop. Maybe she'd end this little sample and let him finish after breakfast, since they were at the spot waiting for them.

ManMan stuck his finger in her ass and sucked on her clit hard. "Shiiiiidddd!" screamed out Ew Baby as he made her knees shake. Ew Baby decided that she would just have to miss breakfast because there was no way she was going to make that nigga stop what he was doing, and when she got a chance to explain things to Lay, she knew that her sis would completely understand.

CHAPTER TEN

*C*raig was out making his end of the night rounds through the neighborhood before he was about to call it a night. He was the person responsible for keeping the properties clean, so he spent a lot of time hitting blocks and being a security guard. His heart was still heavy, because they hadn't found Geechie yet. He was the reason why Cam was dead, and Geechie was the one who directed them niggas to rob his brothers. Word around the neighborhood was that Geechie had gone to Chicago to lay low for a while. Craig had a few cousins and homeboys that stayed up that way, so he placed a call to have them scout out a few spots that Geechie was known to frequent. He instructed them not to kill Geechie, because he wanted to leave that to him and his brothers.

Craig was driving down Annie Malone when he noticed a car that looked like the one Ax had described that the robbers were in. He rode past but wanted to take a closer look. He turned down Cote Brilliant and decided to hit the block once more. He came back around the corner, and by the time he made it to the corner of Cote Brilliant and Billups Avenue, he noticed Ax going to his car. Craig turned the corner expediently and stopped hard on his brakes.

"You got your strap on you?" Craig asked urgently.

"Why would you ask me something foolish like that?" Ax asked, pulling up his shirt.

"Good! Get in!" Craig snapped. "I want you to ride around the corner with me. I think I spotted the car that Geechie was in when they tried to rob y'all." Ax ran around the van and opened the door.

"You should have just said that first," Ax scoffed. Craig pulled off and hit the blocks quickly. When he made it down to the end of the block at Aldine and Annie Malone, the car was still sitting there. Craig turned the corner and pulled up four cars behind the car in question. Ax noticed a few bullet holes in the trunk and bumper, so he knew that it was the getaway car. "That's the car!" Ax hissed angrily.

"Just what I suspected." Craig grimaced, and he instantly called Big Lee's phone.

"Hello," Big Lee answered.

"Hey, little sister. I think we might have found Geechie, and he was right under our noses," Craig explained.

"What! Where you at?" Big Lee questioned.

"I'm on Annie Malone, parked a few cars back from the car they were riding in. I'm wondering if Geechie is up in one of these houses or in the boarding house?" Craig fumed. "I can't wait to get my hands on that nigga!"

"I can't wait either, but don't kill him," Big Lee requested. "I think we should all take part on his demise."

"I agree, and that's why I'm calling you now. Tell Teke to go prepare the basement because we got a live one!" Craig shouted.

"I think we should take him to my warehouse. People will hear his muffled screams in the basement," Big Lee warned.

"That's true," Craig agreed. "I got Ax with me, so call Rico and Ralph and tell them to meet you at the warehouse. I'm gone call Deacon, and we'll meet you as soon as we snatch this nigga up."

"Okay, Craig, in a minute."

A couple of hours had passed, and no one had come out to the car, so Ax had walked down to his house to pick up a few things. He figured that Craig would be able to take Geechie all by himself if he had to, so it cleared him up to go take care of a little business. He hadn't talked to Amanda(Angie) in a few days, so he wondered where she'd been. He walked out of his front door and headed down the steps. He pulled out his phone and decided to call her to see what was up.

"Hi, boo," Angie answered eagerly.

"Hey, you," Ax replied. "Where your ass been? I haven't heard from you in days."

"I've been busy," she replied. "My job has been making me work mandatory overtime, and when I get home, I'm tired."

"You ain't got to work. I'll take care of you," Ax offered.

"That sounds good, but when niggas take care of you, they think they own you," Angie countered.

"I ain't like other niggas," Ax scoffed. "I ain't got to own you, but you'll definitely have to be respectful."

"I'm always respectful and loyal," Angie offered. "I just don't like playing games, that's all."

"So you think this is a game?" Ax questioned.

"I don't know what this is, honestly," she replied sarcastically. "I figured we were just kicking it and enjoying each other's company."

"Is that right?" asked Ax, sounding offended. "Well, what if I said I want more." Angie hesitated for a moment and held the phone. She liked hanging out with Ax, but it would be bad business to fuck around with both Ax and Cecil. "Cat got your tongue?"

"Naw, Axel. A cat doesn't have my tongue, but you got me wondering," Angie admitted.

"You need to leave that nigga alone that you're fucking with in jail and come play with the home team," Ax urged her.

"It sounds good when you say that, but we both know that things change when situations change," Angie countered. "I ain't no sucka for love ass bitch, so the game you spitting may work for most, but on me, you can save that shit for the birds!" Ax laughed as he made it down to Annie Malone.

"Damn, baby, that's cold." He laughed. Ax looked down the street and recognized the jacket one of the men involved in the robbery had on. "Let me call you back in a few. I got some business to handle." Ax hung up the phone before Angie could even respond. He walked up to the back of the van, and Craig noticed the evil grimace that Ax had on his face. He opened the door and climbed inside quickly.

"What do you see, little brother?" Craig asked inquisitively.

"You see that nigga coming down the street? He was one of the niggas that ran up in the garage," Ax explained. Craig pulled one of his work gloves on his hand.

"Well let's get ready to pick us up a nigga!" Craig huffed, putting the other glove on his hand.

"I'm with you, big bro," Ax replied, pulling on his gloves.

The man in question was headed toward the car they had been scoping out. He appeared to be nervous because he kept looking around at his surroundings. He noticed one of Big Lee's work vans sitting a few cars back, so he slowed down his pace a little, trying to see if anyone recognized him. Craig was in the driver's seat, and the back door was open, because they planned on throwing the man in the back of it. Axel had cut through the gangway between two houses, so he could jump out on ole boy from behind. Both brothers were anxious to capture him, because all those niggas were going to pay for Cam's death.

Craig had started up the van as the man approached his car. He looked back in Craig's direction and hit the chirp to pop the locks. He looked around before he got into the car, and that's when Ax came out of nowhere and jumped out on the side of it. He aimed his burner at the dude and smiled smugly at him. Next, Ax ran up on the driver's side and hit the window with his gun. The glass shattered all over the man as he tried to grab his gun out of his waistband. Ax put his burner up to the man's head and smiled.

"Don't even think about it," Ax said as he seethed. "I'll splatter your brains all over this fucking car!"

"Aye, A… A… Ax, man…" the man stuttered. "I wasn't the one who shot your brother. I was the last one to come through the door!"

"But yo' bitch ass was there!" Ax barked back and frowned. "Now hand me your gun and get the fuck out of the car!" The man opened the door, and pieces of glass fell to the floor. "Slowly, nigga! Slowly!" The man pulled his gun out of his waistband and handed it to Ax. Next, he got out of the car and stood with his hands in front of him.

"Don't kill me, Ax! I'm begging you!" the man whined.

"I ain't the one you got to worry about," Ax replied and laughed. "Now come on!"

"Where are we going?"

"On a little ride," Ax replied sarcastically. He and the man walked to the back of the van while Craig looked on.

"What you want me to do, get in the van?" the man stammered nervously.

"Yeah, something like that," Ax replied, hitting the man in the head with the butt of his gun. He clocked him one more time for good measure, and the man went falling down toward the ground. Ax caught him as Craig came to the back of the van to help him. They hurried up and loaded the man's body inside, because it was time for some revenge the Wilson way.

CHAPTER ELEVEN

"What's taking them so long?" Rico complained. "I would have kicked in a few doors a long time ago to find the nigga!"

"No your punk ass wouldn't," Ralph signified and laughed. "Your ass would be waiting for him to come out just like Craig and Ax."

"You's a fucking lie!" Rico snapped with a frown on his face. "I'm not being patient with no nigga that killed my brother! We should have gone and burned down Cecil's mama's house!"

"Now you're talking crazy," Big Lee interjected. "That lady ain't done shit to us! Plus, you know she's off into church. Mrs. Parker don't play with her children, and she always says how she can't believe that I've stayed with Cecil for as long as I have. Besides, Mama would have a fucking fit if we did some shit like that!"

"You got everyone fooled with this bogus marriage, huh?" said Whisper sarcastically.

"Shiiiidddd... You do what you gotta do," Big Lee replied and smirked. They heard the garage door to the warehouse begin to lift up, so everyone turned in that direction. They knew it had to be either Craig or Deacon pulling in. The door made it to the top, and Craig's van pulled inside. "Here we go!" Big Lee shouted enthusiastically.

"It's about damn time," Rico spat. "I'm ready to bust a nigga's head wide open!" Rico hit the crowbar that he was holding against his hand. He wanted to take all of his anger and frustration out on this dude. He was partly responsible for the death of his little brother, and nothing in the world could save him from his fate.

"What took y'all so long?" asked Ralph in an annoyed tone.

"Yeah! What took y'all so got damn long?" Rico shouted.

"We had to wait for the nigga to expose himself," Ax explained, frowning. "We weren't about to do no door to door campaign, nigga!"

"Shit, you should have," Rico scoffed. "It would have saved us some fucking time! I got shit to do, and waiting around for y'all niggas to come was taking forever!"

"Well, we're here now, Rico, so stop all your whining like a little bitch!" Craig huffed. "You get on my nerves with that bullshit."

"Man, fuck what you talking about, Craig. Where that nigga at?" Rico hissed. Craig walked around to the back of the van, and everyone followed behind him. He opened up the door, and everyone stared at the unconscious man. Ax had climbed in the back to duct tape their prisoner. Craig looked around at all of his siblings and called out, "We've got work to do. Let's get it!"

****

"Where you at?" Ax asked anxiously.

"I'm about to go to class. Why, what's up?" Ew Baby asked nonchalantly.

"I need for you to do something for me."

"If I have time," Ew Baby replied. "You know my mama gave me a timeline to finish school and get my license." Ax laughed because he could hear the desperation in Ew Baby's voice.

"I promise it won't take long, and you might need Lay to help you," Ax explained.

"Lay is gone, so she can't help me do shit," Ew Baby informed him. "What is it anyway?"

"I need for you to go pick up a car and take it somewhere for me," Ax told her.

"Whose car is it?" Ew Baby asked then hesitated. "I mean, where am I going?" Ax thought about it for a moment.

"You know what… I shouldn't have called you, my fault," Ax apologized.

"Are you sure?" Ew Baby spoke up.

"Yeah, I'm sure," Ax replied. "Are you busy later?"

"Yeah, I have to go to work. Why don't you come by the lounge to see me?" Ew Baby suggested.

"That sounds like a plan," Ax replied. "I'll see you later. Love you!"

"All right, bye," Ew Baby uttered and smiled. She stared off for a second because he told her that he loved her. She'd been feeling some type of way about Ax lately. They'd been spending more time together since Cam died, and on one night in particular, things got a little intense between them. Ax had been drinking heavily, and he was feeling vulnerable. Ew Baby just so happened to pull up and noticed him sitting on the porch. She got out and went to speak, but she wasn't aware of how intoxicated Ax was until she walked up on him. She convinced him to go into the house, even though he didn't want to go in alone. It didn't feel the same without Cam being around, and his bachelor pad felt empty and lonely. Ew Baby told him that she'd stay for a little while, but she had things to do in the morning.

They went into Ax's house, and things were thrown everywhere. There were empty beer and liquor bottles all over the place. There were empty food containers and random trash all over the living floor and kitchen table. Ew Baby felt sorry for Ax and instantly started cleaning up. Ax went over and crashed on the couch because he was so fucked up. He was so drunk he could barely stand, and it was best that he went to sleep to stay out of Ew Baby's way. She continued to straighten up and get Ax's house back in order. When he woke up, Ew Baby was in the kitchen washing dishes. The house was spotless, and a pile of money was sitting on top of the table. Ax walked into the kitchen, still half buzzed from his binge drinking. He walked up on Ew Baby and pressed his erection against her butt. He thanked her for cleaning up and not stealing from him.

He took a stack of folded bills and slid them down into Ew Baby's bra. Next, he cupped her breasts and grinded his bulge into the crack of her ass in a circular motion. He kissed Ew Baby's neck while he moaned with lustful desires in her ear. Ew Baby tried to stop him, but she wanted it just as much as he did. She'd longed for the day that Ax realized that she was a grown woman and took it upon himself to act on his feelings. They'd fooled around before when she was a teenager, but it never went as far as him sucking her pussy. He used to feel guilty afterward because she was supposed to be his niece. However, he straight dug Ew Baby, and that's why he always kept her so close to him.

****

Ew Baby walked out of the door and noticed her sister Dolly walking down the street. She was supposed to be at school, so Ew Baby couldn't understand what was going on. She put her stuff in the car and then shut the door. She wanted to know what was up with her sister since she had a few minutes to spare.

"Dolly!" yelled Ew Baby loudly. Dolly looked back nervously as Ew Baby came down the street. "Where are you going?"

"I was on my way to the store," Dolly explained. Ew Baby stopped in front of Dolly and stared her down.

"Why ain't you at school?" Ew Baby asked skeptically. "Did that fat muthafucka keep you home from school?"

"Naw, my daddy didn't keep me at home. As a matter of fact, he ain't been there in a few days. I think he got a new woman because I heard him and mama in the back room arguing," Dolly explained.

"Has that muthafucka been trying to touch on you?" Ew Baby probed.

"Nope," Dolly replied. "Mama has been keeping a close eye on me, and that's why I'm at home. She's been sick for the past few days, and that's why I'm on my way to the store to see Deacon with this note." Ew Baby looked at the piece of paper and snatched it out of her hand. She opened it up and saw that Patricia was begging him for drugs. Ew Baby looked at Dolly and shook her head because Big Daddy must be on one and didn't give Patricia no dope.

"Here. Take this note back and hurry up to the store," Ew Baby instructed. She reached down in her pocket and pulled out a few twenty-dollar bills. "Here, take this money and give forty of it to Deacon. Take the other twenty and get some lunchmeat, bread, and a jug of juice. I'll send someone around to the house with a food stamp card for you to go shopping later."

"Mama gave me her card and told me to get some food for the house too," Dolly explained. "Big Daddy has been acting real mean to all of us. Mama said, 'don't pay him any attention,' so we've been ignoring him, but he's been looking at me funny and tried to come into the bathroom one day when I was in the tub. Mama told him to get away from the door, and they started arguing." This angered Ew Baby, because she knew what that meant.

"You keep your phone with you at all times," Ew Baby instructed Dolly. "Do you still have the bat in your room by your bed?"

"Yes, and I have the box cutter that Ms. Lee Ann gave me," Dolly informed her sister.

"When did Mama give you a box cutter?" asked Ew Baby, surprised.

"She gave it to me a few weeks ago when she came to collect the rent money," Dolly replied. "She gave all of us one and told me to use it if that mf'er came near me," Dolly bragged and smiled. "Ms. Lee Ann told Patricia that she better keep us safe, or her ass is going to be gone!" Ew Baby smiled because she appreciated Big Lee for everything that she does for her family.

"Okay, Dolly, I have to go to school." Ew Baby smiled. "I love you."

"I love you too!" Dolly replied. Ew Baby turned to walk off to her car when she saw Craig driving by with the hazardous waste trashcan in the back of his work truck. She did a double take because she saw him in the van earlier. *He must have handled some business; that's why he has that can on the back of the truck.* Ew Baby thought about her conversation with Ax and knew most definitely that some shit had gone down.

CHAPTER TWELVE

*L*ay walked into Big Lee's house to raid her refrigerator. There was always something to eat there, and she was starving. She walked into the kitchen and put her purse down in one of the kitchen chairs. Next, she walked over to the sink and washed her hands. She could hear her mother's voice, and it sounded like she was on the phone. Lay didn't pay it any mind and went over to the refrigerator to grab some food. She opened it up, and a big smile spread across her face. There were Tupperware bowls piled high on the shelf, and this made Lay very happy.

"Why are you holding my refrigerator door open like that?" Big Lee fussed. Lay turned around and smiled at her mother.

"Hi, Mama." Lay giggled, taking some of the containers out.

"Do you ever cook at home?" Big Lee asked, frowning. "You have a man now, so you should be cooking for him."

"I cook for my man, but it's early in the day," Lay explained. "You know you and Whisper ain't gon' eat all of this food, Mama. Quit being stingy." Big Lee laughed at her baby as she took a plate out of the dish drain. She set it on the table and pulled out a chair.

"That was so nice of you to get me a plate." Lay gushed.

"Girl, this plate ain't for you," Big Lee scoffed. "I'm about to fix me a plate, too." Lay laughed as she walked over to the cabinet to get herself a plate. "We caught one of those muthafuckas who killed your uncle last night."

"What! Why didn't y'all call me?" Lay whined. Big Lee looked at her with a stupid expression on her face.

"What was you gon' do, Lay?" Big Lee questioned, curiously.

"I was gon' help beat his ass!" Lay fumed. "I want to get my rocks off on them, too, Mama! You know Cam was my favorite uncle, and those niggas took him from us!"

"I know, baby, but there are some things that you just don't need to be involved in, baby girl," Big Lee explained. "Your uncles and daddy took care of his ass real good. I cracked that nigga's head open like a watermelon with a metal baseball bat, and I cut all of his fingers off."

"Damn, Mama! You put them in your jar, didn't you? I know that shi… I mean stuff looked nasty!" Lay uttered and cringed. Big Lee laughed at her daughter because Lay was real squeamish.

"Yeah, it wasn't pretty, but justice was served in my eyes. Craig put his body in the hazardous waste can and took it to the chop shop. They're going to finish cutting it up and send it down to the pig farmer in Joplin, Missouri," Big Lee explained while she fixed her plate. "Anyway, I have something I want to talk to you about."

"Okay. What's up?" Lay replied cheerfully. She picked up her mother's plate and took it over to the microwave. "How long do you want me to heat up your food?"

"Put it on three minutes so my shit is warmed all the way through,"

Big Lee instructed. She pulled out a cigarette and fired it up. "Lay, I told you that there was some more stuff that I needed to tell you. I think it's time for you to know all of the truth because you're old enough to understand." Lay noticed the serious look on her mother's face, and this worried her, because what else could her mother be hiding from her.

"I don't like the look on your face, Mama." Lay groaned. "Is it something bad?"

"Not really," Big Lee replied. "I wanted you to know that not only is Cecil not your daddy, we're not legally married. I got our marriage annulled a few weeks after it happened." Lay walked over to the microwave when it beeped, and she took her mother's food out of it.

"Well that's good to hear," Lay replied, feeling a bit relieved. "That bastard didn't deserve your hand in marriage anyway, and is you and Whisper going to get married now?" Lay smiled at her mother as she walked her plate over to the microwave.

"I would like to marry my soul mate, but it's totally up to him," Big Lee replied.

"Have you ever thought about proposing to him?" Lay asked curiously.

"Child, Whisper would throw a fit if I asked him to marry me!" Big Lee yelled out and laughed. "We had a discussion about this before, and he said a man is supposed to ask the woman for their hand in marriage."

"So my daddy is a traditionalist?" Lay questioned and giggled. "That sounds funny referring to Whisper as my daddy. I wonder does he want me to call him Daddy." Lay scratched her head and smiled. "I think I'm going to call him Pops!" Big Lee laughed as she took a bite of her food.

"You can call him whatever you want," Big Lee assured her. "He's actually excited about you being his daughter. He said that it always felt like you were his child."

"And I've always felt like he was my father, even though I did try to kiss him," Lay replied frankly. "But I was drunk off my tail!" Lay hunched her shoulders with a nonchalant look on her face. "Is that all you had to tell me?"

"No, there's something else, baby." Big Lee sighed. She put her fork down on her plate and pushed it away. "Now what I'm about to tell you may be a shock, and I've known for the past eight years."

"Do you have cancer?" Lay quaked. Big Lee saw the panic on her baby's face and quickly tried to ease her fears.

"No, Lay," Big Lee assured her. "I don't know how to say it, so I'm just going to tell you. Ew Baby is Cecil's daughter. That's why I took her in when the people came to take her to foster care. Cecil came clean with it and begged me to take her into our family." Lay stared at Big Lee blankly because she didn't know what to say at first. She walked over to the microwave and got her food out. "Are you going to say something?" Lay turned and sat down with her mother. "I know this is a shock to you. How do you feel about it?"

"I guess it is a bit of a shock," Lay uttered. "I kind of knew because I overheard Deacon talking about it with Craig one day, a few years back. Her name is Cecilia, so it made sense to me. I just figured that Ew

Baby was my real sister and you didn't want anyone to know."

"That's the reason why I annulled the marriage. He moved his bitch on our block, and I befriended the hoe! I wondered at first why Cecil was so helpful to Patricia, but he fed me a line about her being his homeboy's chick, and he promised that he'd take care of her and Ew Baby," Big Lee muttered.

"It's all good, Mama. Ew Baby is my sister no matter who's her daddy. She always has my back, and I got hers," Lay declared. "It's just us against the world." Big Lee smiled, because she loved how forgiving her baby was toward her and the mistakes she'd made along the way.

"I love you, little girl," Big Lee declared.

"I love you too, Mama." Lay's phone went off, and a big smile came across her face. She'd given Byrd his own ringtone so she could recognize when he called.

"That must be that nigga," Big Lee teased.

"And you know this." Lay giggled. "I'm going to take this call in the other room."

"I don't care about y'all conversation," Big Lee scoffed. "Y'all ain't talking about shit no way!" Lay laughed at her mother as she walked out of the kitchen. She went into the living room and plopped down on the couch.

"Hello," said Lay in a sexy tone.

"What took you so long to answer the phone?" Byrd questioned authoritatively. "I only have a few minutes between class, and I wanted to hear my baby's voice."

"I was talking to my mama about some stuff," Lay explained.

"Your mama has some stuff to talk about. It's crazy that Whisper's your father."

"Ain't it?" Lay agreed. "I'm still trying to wrap my head around it but get this shit. Why is Cecil, Ew Baby's daddy?"

"What? Put that on something!" Byrd called out. "Man, that's crazy!"

"I know, right!" Lay co-signed and laughed.

"Does she know?" Byrd asked nosily.

"I don't think so," Lay replied. "My mama is going to tell her eventually, I guess. I'm going to ask her when I go back into the kitchen."

"You must be over your mama's house eating." Byrd laughed.

"You know I'm greedy, and there's always leftovers in her fridge," Lay bragged. "I'll be over here every day this week to get something to eat."

"Are you still cooking dinner for me?" Byrd asked curiously.

"It's funny you should say that because my mama just asked if I cook for you." Lay laughed thinking about the coincidence. "I plan on it, and I'm even going to make you dessert."

"That sweet pussy is enough dessert for me." Byrd chuckled.

"You so nasty, Bird." She giggled. "And I like it!"

"I know you do," Byrd uttered arrogantly. He looked at his watch. "Well, baby, I have to go. Tell me you love me."

"Infinitely, baby," Lay replied.

"Infinitely, baby," Byrd replied. "Talk to you after class."

"Okay, baby, bye." Lay hung up the phone and smiled for a few minutes. She loved the direction her relationship with Byrd was going, and she finally let everyone know that he was her man. She heard the microwave go off and remembered that she was about to eat. She got up off the couch and went back into the kitchen to enjoy her afternoon with her mama.

CHAPTER THIRTEEN

A Few Weeks Later

$\mathcal{A}$x and Ew Baby walked into ManMan's house ready to make shit happen. They had gone down on the boat, and their luck wasn't shit! Ax complained that the tables weren't being kind to him, so he decided to go to the hood where he felt confident that he was going to hit. Ew Baby noticed that he'd been wiping his nose a lot, but she figured that he must have a cold or something because this was out of the norm for Ax.

"Hey, Ewwww Baby," ManMan spoke. He pulled her into his arms and planted a kiss on her lips.

"Hey, ManMan." She blushed. Ax looked at ManMan, and an instant rage came across him.

"What you all up in her face for?" Ax hissed. "The last time I checked, you was all up in Layloni's face!"

"It's cool, Ax," Ew Baby assured him. "Me and ManMan have been rocking for a minute now, and he's no longer obsessed with my sister. Ain't that right, baby?"

"Yeah, that's right," ManMan replied. "Why you busting my balls,

Ax? I thought we were cool."

"We are cool, but let a nigga know what's going on," Ax replied agitated. He looked at Ew Baby and didn't like what he saw. He never liked seeing her with any man, but this particular one was really unnerving. "Can you go get me something to drink, Ew Baby?"

"Sure. What do you want?" she asked.

"You know what I like," Ax scoffed. ManMan noticed the way that Ax was looking at her, and it wasn't the way an uncle looks at a niece.

"I'll be right back," Ew Baby replied. Both men watched as she walked away from them. Ax quickly moved in closer to ManMan and stared him up and down.

"I bet not hear about you putting your hands on her or breaking her heart," Ax seethed. "'Cause you know I'll fuck you up!"

"Damn, Ax. A nigga ain't gon' do shit to Ew Baby," ManMan replied defensively. "I actually like your niece. She's hella cool and a down ass bitch."

"Who's a bitch?" Ax snapped. ManMan panicked for a second because Ax looked like he was about to pounce.

"I didn't mean anything derogatory or nothing like that," ManMan explained. "I'm just saying, she's a cool ass young lady." Ax glared at ManMan for a second then fell out laughing.

"You should see your face!" Ax laughed. "I'm just fucking with you, but I am serious, though!" Ew Baby walked back up and handed Ax his cup.

"Are you over here threatening him, Ax?" Ew Baby asked defensively.

"Now you know I'm not doing nothing, Ew Baby," Ax assured her. "I'm about to go hit one of these tables, so if you'll excuse me." He winked at Ew Baby and walked off.

"Maaaaan… your uncle is a trip!" ManMan uttered. "If I didn't know any better, I'd think he was jealous."

"That's ridiculous," Ew Baby replied. "He's just overprotective of me. Ever since Cam died, he's been having a bit of a rough time. You know that was his best friend in the whole wide world."

"If you say so, Ew Baby, but I saw the way he looked at you," ManMan explained. "And it's the same way that I look at you." ManMan put his arm around Ew Baby's waist. "You off tonight?"

"As a matter of fact, I'm not. I told this nigga to drop me off at the lounge, but he insisted on bringing me here," Ew Baby complained.

"Is that a bad thing?" ManMan questioned.

"It all depends." She smiled. "Can you take me around the corner?"

"I sure can, but give me a minute though. I have something to take care of first." ManMan kissed her neck and walked off toward the steps. She noticed how Big Daddy was staring at her, so she rolled her eyes hard at him and settled them on Ax. A smile came across her face because she thought about what ManMan had just said. She wondered how Ax was looking at her, and maybe ManMan was just tripping. She decided to walk over to the table and watch Ax shoot dice. She had twenty minutes to get to work before Big Lee would start blowing up her phone.

Lay was serving customers when she just so happened to look out of the window and saw ManMan's truck pull up in front of the lounge. She watched as Ew Baby leaned over and gave him a kiss before she got out. A frown came over Lay's face because she didn't like Ew Baby messing with ManMan. They'd gone out on a few double dates, and ManMan spent all of his time staring and trying to direct his conversation at Lay. She felt like the only reason why he was messing with Ew Baby was because he was still trying to get close to her.

Ew Baby pranced into the lounge with her gold fronts gleaming, with a big-tooth smile. She went behind the bar and smiled at Lay smugly, because of the weird look Lay had on her face. She knew that Lay felt some type of way about her dating ManMan, but she didn't care. She felt like he finally realized that she was a winner, and maybe Lay was jealous because ManMan wasn't paying her any attention.

"Why you looking at me like that?" Ew Baby asked defensively.

"Looking at you like what?" Lay replied dryly.

"Like I got shit on my face or something." Ew Baby huffed.

"Maybe I'm looking at you like that because you're forty-five minutes late," Lay shot back. "I had to handle these people by myself, and you're supposed to be bar backing for me. It's two for one, and you know we get slammed on a Thursday night!"

"Well I'm sorry, Lay! I got jammed up as usual with—"

"With who? I know you're not about to say ManMan, because shouldn't no nigga keep you from your money," Lay interrupted.

"First of all, it wasn't ManMan who had me late for work; it was Ax! He had me over at the gambling house and didn't want to stop shooting to bring me to work," Ew Baby explained in a stank tone. "It sounds like you got a problem with me fucking with ManMan."

"I ain't got a problem with it. I could give a fuck less about whom you mess with, but for the record, I think it's stupid for you to fuck with ManMan. He used to sweat the shit out of me and you know it, but I guess it doesn't matter because Ew Baby is finally getting some attention."

"Damn, Lay!" Ew Baby laughed. "The hate is real! I can't believe you of all people would say some shit like that to me. I thought you would be happy for me, but I guess I was the fool, huh?"

"The thing you're being a fool about is that nigga you're swooning over! Ew Baby, you know I ain't jealous of this fuckery, so you can keep that shit to yourself! I'm just telling you how I feel because we're supposed to be able to do that! I didn't know I was going to strike a nerve," Lay replied smugly.

"You ain't struck shit here!" Ew Baby frowned.

"What the fuck is going on?" Big Lee snapped. "I got customers complaining about you two up here arguing, and they can't get no drinks! And if they can't get any drinks, I ain't making no money, and that's a problem!"

"We ain't arguing," Lay scoffed. "I was just telling—"

"I don't give a fuck about what you was telling! I'm telling you to cut this shit out and wait on my muthafuckin' customers!" Big Lee interrupted. "And Ew Baby, your ass was forty-five minutes late! You know we get slammed on Thursday evenings! That's why I have your ass come in early to bar back for Lay!"

"I'm sorry, Mama, but Ax had me up in the—"

"You can keep your excuses because I don't give a fuck, Ew Baby! Excuses are like assholes, and everybody got one! You get your ass here on time, or you can go find somewhere else to work!" Big Lee shouted angrily. Lay had already gone back to waiting on customers while Big Lee cursed Ew Baby out. She could tell that Ew Baby was pissed because their mother had just embarrassed them in front of the entire bar.

"Big Lee, you didn't have to cuss that girl out like that," Deacon grumbled.

"Deacon, you shut the fuck up because nobody was talking to your ass anyway!" Big Lee fussed. "This my shit, and if you don't like the ambiance, then get the fuck out! And that goes for any other muthafucka that got something to say!"

"See, you ain't even have to talk to me like that," Deacon scoffed. "And I would be offended if you weren't my sister, but I'm use to you cussing me out, so my feelings ain't even hurt!" Deacon took a sip of his drink then looked up at Big Lee with a big smile on his face. She cut her eyes at him and he broke out laughing.

"You make me sick, Deacon!" Big Lee smirked, trying to conceal her smile.

"I love you too, sis! Now carry your ass around there and make me a drink to say you're sorry," Deacon insisted. Big Lee didn't say a word. She just walked around to the back of the bar and made her big brother a drink.

CHAPTER FOURTEEN

*B*ig Lee let Lay go early because she could see the tension between she and Ew Baby building. They hadn't said a word to each other since the argument, which bothered Big Lee. She couldn't have her girls mad at each other, because sisters shouldn't stay mad at each other. Lay had always acted like a big sister and often told Ew Baby how she felt, even if it hurt her feelings. She didn't like the fact that Ew Baby was messing around with ManMan, but it wasn't her choice to make. Lay had to understand that Ew Baby had longed to receive genuine love from a man. She never really knew her father, and the one she did know molested her. Big Lee felt like it was time to have a talk with Ew Baby so they could set some things straight. She hoped that Ew Baby wouldn't freak out about what she was about to tell her. She'd already cussed the girl out earlier, and Ew Baby's feelings have been on her sleeve ever since.

"Damn, I'm tired," Big Lee groaned, sitting down on her stool. "Can you give me a bottle of water, please?"

"Yes, ma'am," Ew Baby uttered. She walked over to the small refrigerator and grabbed a bottle of water out of it. She took it over to Big Lee and put it down in front of her. "Mama, I'm sorry for being late. I told Ax that I had to go to work, but he insisted on taking me with him."

"I don't know why you keep getting in the car with Ax when you know you have to come to work." Big Lee chuckled. "'Cause you know he's not going to care."

"I know, Mama, but I just be watching his back," Ew Baby admitted. "He's been acting strange to me, and I just want to make sure he's cool." Big Lee fired up a cigarette as she studied Ew Baby's face.

"Are you fucking my brother?" asked Big Lee frankly. Ew Baby looked at her mother in shock. She was surprised by her words.

"No, ma'am!" Ew Baby quickly answered. "He's like my—"

"Before you fix your mouth to say what you're going to say, no he's not!" Big Lee corrected her. "You don't think I see the way my brother looks at you, Ew Baby?"

"Looks at me like what?" Ew Baby asked with a confused look on her face. She didn't want to talk about Ax with Big Lee because she didn't know what was going on between them. However, if it was becoming obvious to her mother, then she knew she wasn't tripping. Ax had pulled her into the bathroom and tongued her down before ManMan brought her to work. He had gone upstairs to get something, and Ax seized the moment. He told Ew Baby that he loved her and that she needed to leave ManMan alone. She tried to laugh it off, but Ax wouldn't let her. He expressed how he cared about her and that he didn't want no nigga going up in her in no shape, form, or fashion.

"Don't play with me, little girl!" Big Lee fussed. "He done already told me that he likes you."

"What! Are you serious, Mama?" Ew Baby gushed. Big Lee looked at her crossly and frowned.

"Take that cheesy ass grin off your face!" Big Lee scoffed. "I don't know how I feel about this, because you're my daughter and he's my brother."

"To be honest with you, Mama, I don't know how I feel about it either. Ax has never really treated me like I'm his niece when we're not around other people. It's like he puts up a front for everyone, but when we're alone…" Ew Baby stared at Big Lee blankly.

"I want you to tell me the truth, and I promise I won't be mad at you. Have you ever fucked Axel?" asked Big Lee sternly. Ew Baby looked her mother square in the eyes and swallowed hard.

"No, ma'am. I've never screwed Axel; on my dead uncle Killer Cam!" Ew Baby swore. "Now we've kissed and touched each other a couple of times, but that's it!" Big Lee looked at Ew Baby accusingly. "And this happened last year after I turned twenty-one. He always said that I was too young for him to fuck with, but once I came of age, he was going to make me his chick," Ew Baby lied, but she couldn't tell her mother the whole truth because she would be mad. Big Lee put her cigarette out in the water bottle because she had heard just about enough.

"All I have to say is…" She looked up at Ew Baby with a serious look on her face. "It's your life. If you love my brother and want to be with him, then you have my blessing. You know that people are going to talk, but fuck them! Their opinions don't mean shit!"

"Love! Who said anything about love?" Ew Baby frowned. "I mean, I like Ax and all, but—"

"Don't do my brother, little girl," Big Lee interrupted her. "You know you like Axel, so don't even play with me! That's why you keep letting his ass make you late for work!" Ew Baby laughed as she hit Big Lee's hand. ManMan walked through the door and smiled at Ew Baby as he approached the bar. "Here comes this clown ass nigga," Big Lee scoffed then frowned. Ew Baby scrunched her nose up.

"Mama!" Ew Baby called out, embarrassed.

"Hey, Ew Baby," said ManMan enthusiastically. He was high as giraffe pussy and reeked of weed. "How you doing this evening, Big Lee?"

"High," she replied dryly. "From the smell of you!" ManMan and Ew Baby laughed.

"I'll throw you a bag if you want," ManMan offered. Big Lee frowned at ManMan as if she were offended.

"I don't trust light-skinned people," Big Lee confessed. "Y'all some sneaky muthafuckas, and I don't trust you!" She got up off her stool and straightened out her shirt.

"Damn that's cold, Big Lee!" ManMan moaned.

"So is a hoe's heart, so get over it!" Big Lee shot back. She grabbed her cigarettes off the bar and turned to walk away. "Ew Baby, you can go ahead and go; lock the door behind you when you leave. Whisper, Rico, and Ralph are on the other side, so I'm cool."

"All right, Mama," Ew Baby called out. "Was there something else you wanted to talk to me about?"

"It can wait until tomorrow." Big Lee sighed. "I've already confessed my sins enough for today." Ew Baby and ManMan laughed as Big Lee disappeared down the corridor. She figured that telling her about Cecil could wait. She'd waited eight years to get to this point, and one more day wouldn't kill her.

****

Lay had gone home because it was the first of the month, and Byrd was on an all-nighter. He knew that the community was going to be in a constant need of product, and he wanted to keep the people happy. She had a paper due, so skipping on a night to hang out with her sweetie was okay. She was sitting at the kitchen table working on her laptop when Ew Baby and ManMan came into the house. She looked up and saw them then put her head back down in a book she was reading.

"Aye, Lay! Come smoke this blunt with us," Ew Baby called out.

"Naw, I'm cool," Lay replied. Ew Baby walked up to the table and frowned at Lay.

"I know you're not still mad about earlier," Ew Baby uttered. "'Cause if I ain't still mad, then you certainly shouldn't be." Lay looked up at Ew Baby and narrowed her eyes.

"I was never mad, sweetie," Lay replied. "And I have to finish this paper because it's due tomorrow morning."

"More reason to get your mind right so you can write a dope ass paper," Ew Baby countered. Lay could tell that she'd been drinking, and it was obvious that she was in a good mood.

"Honestly, I can't." Lay sighed. "I have to write a ten-page paper, and I only have three pages done." Ew Baby looked at Lay smugly.

"Is it because ManMan's here?" Ew Baby scoffed with an attitude. Lay frowned at Ew Baby because she didn't feel like getting into the bullshit again.

"That has nothing to do with nothing," Lay assured her. "I just have to finish this paper."

"Yeah, alright," Ew Baby hissed. "Let that be the reason!" She rolled her eyes and walked away from the table. Lay started to respond to her smart-ass comment, but she decided not to feed into it.

"Come on, ManMan, let's go! This bitch in here acting brand new and shit!" Ew Baby fumed.

"What did you say?" Lay snapped. She jumped up from her chair and walked into the living room. "Because the only bitch I see standing in here is you, dumb bitch!" Ew Baby turned and scowled at Lay.

"Ain't shit dumb about me, bitch! You're the dummy who didn't want people to know that Byrd was your man. Now how dumb is that? He's the hottest nigga in the hood, and you act like you're too good for him! Tell me, sister, is anyone good enough for Princess Layloni Wilson?"

"To an average bitch like you, that statement would strike a chord, but let's be honest. You wish you were me, don't you? Is that why you're so eager to suck ManMan's dick? He probably pretends like you're me to make himself happy!"

"I ain't got shit to do with this, so keep me out of it!" ManMan interjected. "I'm an innocent party in this, and for the record, I actually like Ew Baby!"

"Sure you do," Lay replied sarcastically, crossing her arms in front of her.

"You conceited bitch!" Ew Baby shouted angrily.

"So! I don't give a fuck what you think about me! As a matter of fact, get the fuck out of my house since you think I'm such a conceited bitch," Lay shouted.

"You can't put me out! This is just as much my house as it is yours!" Ew Baby retorted. "You know that Mama—"

"Mama ain't got shit to do with this! The only reason why my mama took you in was because Cecil begged her to do it!" Ew Baby looked at Lay funny.

"What the fuck is you talking about? Why would Cecil ask Mama to take me in?" Ew Baby questioned, feeling confused. "He ain't got shit to do with shit!"

"That's where you're wrong, dear heart! Cecil's your daddy, and he begged my mama to take you in so that you wouldn't have to stay in a group home. How about that tea?" Lay snapped smugly. A look of disbelief came across Ew Baby's face. How is it that Lay knew that Cecil was her father, but she didn't? Why did Big Lee feel the need to tell Lay, but not her?

"You're lying! You're just saying shit to try to piss me off!" Ew Baby insisted.

"You've been drove since earlier," Lay scoffed. "That was just the cherry on top of the sundae."

"You really are a bitch," ManMan uttered. Lay looked over at him and narrowed her eyes.

"You get the fuck up out of here, too! And take this thot with you!" Lay snapped. "I told this hoe that I don't trust light-skinned niggas, and she insists on bringing you around me!" Tears filled up in Ew Baby's eyes because she was absolutely furious with Lay. She felt like Lay didn't give a fuck about her, and it was obvious that she really didn't care about her feelings. They'd always had little arguments here and there, but that was what sisters did, but were they really sisters for real? Ew Baby felt like ever since Lay found out that Whisper was her father, she'd been acting differently.

"I'm gon' get the fuck out of your house, but I'll be back in the morning to get my shit!" Ew Baby retorted.

"That's fine with me. Just make sure you leave your keys on the table," Lay shot back. "Better yet, the locks will be changed by noon." Ew Baby didn't care to say anything back. All she wanted to do was get away from Lay before she teed off on her. Ew Baby grabbed her purse and jacket and walked toward the door. ManMan was already standing there and opened it up so that they could leave.

Ew Baby put her jacket on as she walked out of the door. She tried to slam it off the hinges as it made a loud thunderous sound that caused the doorframe to shake a little bit. Lay covered her face as tears streamed down her cheeks. It was then that she realized all the mean things she had said to Ew Baby, and she felt bad. She was pissed off at her best friend/sister because she felt like Ew Baby was showing off for ManMan. She knew their relationship was a joke, and for the life of her, she couldn't understand why Ew Baby couldn't see it for what it was. Lay wiped her eyes and went back over to the table. She sat down in the chair and tried to get back to writing her paper, but her emotions were all over the place.

She just sat there and cried because she'd fucked up yet again with her stank ass attitude.

****

Ew Baby walked down the steps quickly to get in ManMan's truck. She didn't want to look like a punk, so she held in her tears. She felt like Lay fronted her out in front of ManMan, and when Lay said that Cecil was her father in front of him, it really made her feel dumb.

"You cool?" ManMan asked, hitting his chirp to open the doors to his truck.

"Yeah, I'm cool." Ew Baby sniffled. "I just want to hit that blunt."

"That's cool," ManMan replied, getting into his truck. "We can smoke this blunt then I have to bounce." Ew Baby frowned up at him.

"What the fuck you mean?" Ew Baby snapped. "I just got put out of my own fucking house because of you, and you're talking about you got to bounce! Nigga, I'm going with you!"

"No the fuck you're not!" ManMan chuckled. "You're the one who decided to pick a fight with Lay. She's always complaining about me being around, so I'm used to it." Ew Baby continued to stare at him in disbelief. "What I didn't know was how much of a bitch Lay was! I mean... I thought it was just an act, but she's a real live bitch! I don't see how Byrd puts up with that shit."

"You're a real bitch ass nigga!" Ew Baby hissed.

"What the fuck did you say to me?" ManMan frowned, grabbing Ew Baby by her hair. "Bitch, I'll beat the fuck out of you! I ain't none of Layloni!"

"Let me go!" Ew Baby screamed, trying to get away from ManMan. She swung her hand and slapped ManMan across the face.

"Bitch, you got me fucked up!" ManMan fumed before he hit Ew Baby in the face. She dug her fingernails into his cheek and brought it down hard, tearing the skin on his cheek. He let her hair go, and Ew Baby swung at him several times, landing a few solid punches. He had Ew Baby fucked up if he thought she was going to let him beat on her. She reached backward for the door handle and grabbed it, but not before ManMan punched her several times in the face. She felt blood gush from her nose as she pushed open the door. ManMan already had the truck running, so he put it in gear as he tried to grab for Ew Baby's hair again. He took off from his parking spot, and Ew Baby fell backward out of his truck. She hit the ground hard and rolled over to the curb. ManMan continued to gun his engine down the street as Ew Baby laid in the gutter, crying.

CHAPTER FIFTEEN

*L*ay couldn't sleep because she was worried about Ew Baby. She couldn't believe that they let things get carried away, and all she wanted to do was say she was sorry. She managed to get her paper done, but she didn't feel confident about it. She was so distracted, and Byrd was too busy to talk to her, so she decided to go make her a cup of coffee to go along with her blunt. She and Ew Baby used to call it the breakfast of champions; wake and bake Ew Baby liked to say.

Lay was in the kitchen and started making herself a single cup of coffee when she heard the alarm beep, alerting her that someone was coming through the front door. She figured it was Ew Baby coming to get her stuff, and she wanted to apologize for how ugly she acted. Everyone has been so stressed out here lately, and Lay just wanted her sister to know she only had good intentions toward her that went terribly, terribly wrong.

Ew Baby came through the door and tried to shut it quietly because she didn't want to run into Lay. She'd slept in her car because she felt she couldn't come back in the house, and it was too late for her to go anywhere else. More importantly, she didn't want anyone to see her face. She opened up her purse and started searching for her phone when Lay's reaction made her look up, a bit startled.

"What the fuck happened to your face!" Lay shouted in horror.

"Why do you care?" Ew Baby retorted. "I don't mean shit to you!" A hard frown came across Lay's mouth as she observed the dried-up blood on Ew Baby's face and jacket. Also, she noticed a big ass knot on her head where it looked like she'd been hit with something. Lay charged toward Ew Baby and grabbed her by the jacket because she wasn't about to take too much more of Ew Baby's smart-ass mouth!

"Don't fucking play with me, Ew Baby! What the fuck happened to your face!" Lay yelled. Ew Baby looked up at Lay with tears in her eyes. She wanted to play tough, but her heart felt heavy. She felt like she was alone in the world, because the one person that she loved the most put her out. Tears welled up in Lay's eyes as anger and hurt filled her heart. "You tell me who did this to you! You tell me right now!"

"Nobody did this to me. I did this to myself by being stupid," Ew Baby stammered. "As usual, you were right about ManMan, and he didn't wait to prove you wrong. We got into an argument, and I called him a bitch ass nigga because he tried to one-two on me once we got into the truck. All of a sudden, he had something to do and said I couldn't go with him. I believe the only reason why he did that was because he heard you put me out."

"ManMan did this to your face?" Lay fumed.

"Yes, but I fucked him up! His pink ass is going to have permanent marks on his face from me digging my nails down into his cheek! I tried to take all the skin off the side of that muthafucka!" Ew Baby cried. She started to laugh when she thought about something that happened. "He tried to hold on to me when he pulled off because my door was open, but I jumped up out of that thang and fucked myself up. I'm a little sore, and I have a lump on my head, but I'm good." Lay grabbed Ew Baby and pulled her into her arms then hugged her tightly.

"I'm sorry, Ew Baby. I said some mean and hurtful things to you last night, and I feel so bad about it. I really was being a real bitch, and I'm—"

"You're sorry?" Ew Baby interrupted. "I was poppin' off at the mouth too, and I probably deserved some of it, but why would you yell out that Cecil was my father... and in front of ManMan? That was some private shit that you should have said to me when we were alone."

"I don't know," Lay confessed. "I guess I was so mad I let my anger get the best of me, and you're right. I should have said those things to you in private; better yet, I should have never said those things to you." Ew Baby snatched away from Lay.

"I'm still mad at you, so don't go getting all lovey dovey on me. This ain't the first time a nigga has beat on me." Ew Baby was seething as she frowned. Lay looked at Ew Baby sternly.

"And we gon' handle that nigga like we did the last muthafucka that put his hands on you," Lay retorted angrily. She put her hand on the side of Ew Baby's face. "Now go take a hot bath and relax. I'll be up in a few minutes with a little wake and bake and a bag of frozen vegetables." She held out the blunt that she was holding, and Ew Baby looked down at her hand smugly. "I know you're mad at me, but don't make me beat your ass, too!" Ew Baby smirked as she snatched the blunt out of Lay's hand.

"Do we have some of that lavender bubble bath?" Ew Baby

mumbled.

"No, but we have that one with shea butter. You should put some Epsom salt in your bathwater as well because I know your ass is aching. ManMan's truck sits pretty high up off the ground, so that fall you took had to hurt." Ew Baby looked at Lay and smirked.

"My ass tucked and rolled," Ew Baby joked. "You should have seen how my ass bounced and rolled over into the gutter!" A smile came across Lay's face as Ew Baby broke out into an infectious laugh. Lay tried to hold her composure, but she couldn't keep from laughing. Ew Baby hugged Lay because she loved her sister, then walked up the steps to her room. Lay watched as Ew Baby disappeared down the hall, before an evil grimace came across her face. She was going to get that high-yellow muthafucka ManMan, and he was going to be sorry that he put his hands on Ew Baby.

****

"Are you sure?" Byrd asked, pissed. "Okay, baby, calm down. I'll be around there later to take you to school." He hung up the phone and pinched the bridge of his nose. He was sitting on the couch and had just woke up when his bae called with this bullshit. Lay had told him what ManMan did to Ew Baby, and she was ready to go kill him with her bare hands. He didn't condone men beating on women because his father always taught him that a real man walks away from an angry woman, no matter if they hit you or not. He wondered what had happened to ManMan's face when he came into the trap house last night. He told Byrd that he walked into some tree branches, but Byrd knew that he was lying by the way his wounds looked.

ManMan came from the back with two plates of food in his hand. Mara, one of the women who lived in the house they trapped out of, cooked breakfast for them. Byrd had been going hard all night because if niggas found out that he was sitting on some weight, they would have conversation for the drug agents when they ass got picked up. Byrd had spent two nights away from Lay, and he was truly missing her warm body lying next to his. However, he was a little disturbed by what she'd just told him, and he wanted to get to the bottom of the situation.

"Aye… what's this I hear about you jumping on Ew Baby?" Byrd asked frankly.

"Man, fuck that bitch! She scratched my fucking face up!" ManMan said as he seethed.

"I thought you said some tree branches did that shit to your face. I knew your ass was lying!" Byrd shot back. ManMan looked up from his plate of food and glared at Byrd, annoyed.

"What, you mad or something? I didn't know you were fucking Ew Baby, too! I bet that threesome was righteous," ManMan replied sarcastically.

"You got jokes, huh?" Byrd questioned with a frown on his face. "I ain't fucking Ew Baby, but I think it's fucked up that you beat on a woman. Only a bitch ass nigga would put their hands on a female. She couldn't have possibly hurt you that bad that you had to put bruises on her face."

"Look at my fucking face! This shit hurts, and I think it's going to leave a permanent scar!" ManMan hissed. "That bitch had to have flesh in her nails on top of the skin that she peeled off my shit!"

"That ain't all you gon' have after her mama and uncles find out that you put your hands on her," Byrd uttered sarcastically. "You know they're already on a mission, trying to find Geechie, so you just might have signed your death certificate, bruh!" ManMan looked at him smugly.

"I ain't scared of them! I got guns, too," ManMan boasted. "And I got peoples too! If they try to come at me, I'm just gon' handle their asses accordingly."

"You talking heavy as fuck, but you know your ass is a punk," Byrd replied and laughed.

"What did you just say to me, bitch ass nigga?" ManMan retorted. Byrd smiled at ManMan because he was in his feelings.

"You heard me, ole weak ass nigga!" Byrd spat. "You must have forgotten, I know you's a punk ass dude! You talk heavy, but you ain't about that life. How many bodies you got, ManMan?" ManMan looked at him stupidly, because Byrd was right. He knew that he couldn't hold a candle to Byrd, because Byrd had put in a lot of work for their crew. Whenever someone posed or made a threat against them, Byrd was one of the ones who handled the static. He always did his dirt alone and never told anyone what he'd done; it was safer that way.

"You ain't all that heavy yourself, Byrd Man! Ain't nobody ever heard of you putting in work either," ManMan mentioned.

"That's because I'm smarter than all of you," Byrd replied and laughed. "You think I'd tell a bunch of chitter chatter ass niggas the shit that I've done? I'd be locked up somewhere because you niggas talk worse than bitches."

"Fuck you, Byrd! Ever since we found out that you fuck with Lay, you've been acting like you're better than us! I'm guessing that her mommy threw you a bone, and that's why you've been up doing all nighters for the past few days," ManMan scoffed. "I guess Big Lee's got her titty in your mouth, too!" Byrd glared over at ManMan angrily.

"Huh?" Byrd scoffed. "Big Lee ain't got shit in my mouth! However, I do enjoy the taste of her daughter's pussy, something your weak ass always dreams about every night. See, that's your problem, ManMan. You're always worried about the next man, when you should be focused on yourself. You got the gambling house and you hustle, so what I got going on shouldn't even bother you. I thought you were the man." A smug smile came across Byrd's face because he'd just shut his best friend down. "I guess I was mistaken." ManMan glared at Byrd because, in all actuality, he was jealous as hell of Byrd. He had Lay as his girl, and that was all that ManMan ever wanted. It was true that he was pursuing her to help out Cecil, but he had a lust for her that grew deep inside. He knew that having Lay by his side as his chick, he'd be on top of the world. Everyone in the city would finally know who he was because he would have the Wilson Family name behind him, and that name alone holds power.

"Whatever, nigga," ManMan scoffed. "I am the fucking man, and your ass knows it's true!"

"Yeah, I know." Byrd chuckled. "But I also know that you're a bitch ass nigga!" ManMan had finally gotten completely pissed off. He threw his plate of food down on the floor and jumped up off the couch. Byrd looked down at the scattered food all over the floor then he looked up at ManMan and smiled.

"What you wanna do, ManMan?" Byrd asked before taking a bite of his toast. "I know you don't want these hands." ManMan stared vehemently down at Byrd because his arrogance was starting to show, and ManMan didn't like it.

"Nigga, you better watch yourself! You ain't untouchable." ManMan was seething.

"This is true," Byrd agreed. "But I bet your weak ass ain't gon' do shit!" Byrd continued to eat his breakfast as he stared at his best friend smugly. "Now go get something to clean this shit up. You just wasted some perfectly good food."

"Clean the shit up yourself!" ManMan retorted. "I got shit to do!" He turned and walked toward the back of the house and went out the back door. Byrd continued to eat his food as he pondered over the argument he'd just had with ManMan. They used to be really close, but here lately, shit had been going left between them. Byrd could tell that ManMan was jealous of him because of Lay, and he'd need to keep a close eye on his best friend because a jealous nigga was a telling nigga.

CHAPTER SIXTEEN

"*H*ello," Angie whispered.

"Why you whispering in the phone?" asked Cecil irritably. Angie had been ignoring his phone calls for the past few days, and this had pissed Cecil off.

"I'm at my parent's house, and I didn't want to disturb them," Angie explained. "My grandmother has been sick, so I've been up at the hospital with them. That's why I'm whispering in the phone."

"Your brother told me that she was sick. How is she doing?" Cecil asked.

"She's doing better. The doctor said she might be coming home in a few days," Angie explained.

"That's a good thing," Cecil replied. "Has Geechie contacted you since he's been gone? You know I'll be home in two months, and I need to know where that nigga is, so that we can put together our plan." Angie didn't respond to Cecil, and this pissed him off. She'd been acting brand new for the past few weeks, and he wondered if Ax had her nose wide open. "Did you hear me, Angie?"

"Oh, I'm sorry! What did you say?" Angie mumbled. She was looking through a crack in the bathroom door at Ax. He was sleep when she got out the bed to answer the phone, but it looked like he was wide-awake now. She couldn't pay attention to Cecil's conversation, because she was too busy watching Ax snort something up his nose. She had her suspicions that it was more than just an occasional thing, but to actually see him constantly doing drugs, made her stomach upset. "I think I have a way for us to come up," Angie interrupted Cecil. "Do you trust me, Cecil?"

"Yeah, I trust you, Angie. That's why I'm so irritated by how you've been carrying me for these past few weeks," Cecil complained. "It's apparent that some nigga must have your attention, and he's throwing you off your game!"

"I must admit to you, there is a certain gentleman friend that's been occupying my time," Angie admitted. "But the reward is going to be so lucrative for the both of us, that you'll forgive me for my absence."

"I know who it is, and are you fucking that nigga?" Cecil questioned.

"I don't think you should be questioning me about my infidelities. Are you still fucking my brother?" Angie scoffed.

"Don't play with me, Angie!" Cecil snapped. "You know that I'm all about you!"

"I guess now you are," Angie uttered then giggled. "Because at first you were all about my brother, that's how we hooked up in the first place, remember?"

"I don't appreciate you implying that I'm a fag like your brother," Cecil fumed. "I got a whole wife at home, so what I look like fucking with a fag? Big Lee would kill me if she heard some shit like that!"

"I doubt it," Angie scoffed. "She's pretty occupied with that fine ass nigga, Whisper. Did you know that he's actually your daughter Lay's daddy?"

"How do you know?" asked Cecil urgently. "Who told you that?"

"Let's just say a little birdie told me, and from what I understand, it didn't even make a wave in their relationship. As a matter of fact, it seemed like it made their bond even stronger," Angie gloated.

"Damn! I was going to continue to exploit Lee's ass with that tad bit of information. I was able to get a lot of shit done by holding that over her head," Cecil said in a miffed tone. "And since Geechie went and pulled that bullshit, Lee hasn't taken any of my calls. She sent a message that she's going to spare my life, but Geechie was as good as dead!"

"And she's serious, too!" Angie conveyed. "All three of the niggas that were in on the robbery with Geechie are dead. One nigga was found hanging from the tree, beaten with his throat slashed, and the other two are missing. Geechie said that one of his boys never made it out of the garage, so you know they got rid of the body."

"Damn!" Cecil shouted. The guard looked over at him as Cecil returned his gaze. He threw his hand up to signify that everything was all right. "Look, I'm gone need you to be on point. I can't afford to lose you, Angie. You've been a great help to me, and I promise that it's going to get greater later."

"You don't have to worry, Cecil. I'm not going anywhere," Angie assured him. Ax got up and stretched then turned and headed toward the bathroom. "Look, I got to go. Call me later on in the week." She hung up the phone before Cecil could get a word out edgewise. She placed her phone down on the sink and turned on the shower.

"Who were you in here talking too?" Ax asked, staring at her.

"I was just touching base with my mama to see how my granny was doing today," Angie explained. "The doctor said that she might be able to come home in a couple of days."

"That's great news, baby," Ax replied plainly. He wrapped his arms around Angie and looked down into her eyes. She noticed a little bit of white powder on the corner of Ax's nose, and this bothered her. She took her hand and wiped it off as she continued to stare into Ax's eyes. She really liked hanging out with him because they always had a lot of fun. However, the other day she'd seen him and Ew Baby riding down MLK. She didn't know who Ew Baby was for sure, but that wasn't the first time she'd seen them together.

"So you like to tweak your nose, huh?" asked Angie judgmentally.

"I told you that I bump a lil', but it ain't nothing serious." Ax frowned. "I can stop whenever I want too." Angie looked at him skeptically.

"If you say so, Axel," she replied. "Most dope heads say the same thing, and months from now, you'll be walking around here snotted out of your mind."

"I ain't like other niggas," Ax replied. "I can handle myself, so you don't have to worry."

"Should I worry about that girl I keep seeing you with?" Angie asked skeptically.

"What girl?" Ax wondered. "I ain't got no woman, so I don't know who you're talking about."

"I'm talking about the brown skinned girl with the long platinum weave that I've seen you with a couple of times," Angie explained. Ax looked at her puzzled for a minute.

"Are you talking about Ew Baby? She ain't nobody to worry about," Ax assured her. "That's my sidekick and you know I told you about her!" A big smile came across his face as he noticed a hint of jealousy on Angie's face.

"Your sidekick, huh?" Angie scoffed. "So is that the new term for other bitches you're fucking?" Ax laughed as he gripped Angie's butt cheeks.

"Ew Baby is my sister's foster daughter. I told you about her! She's been my right hand man since forever, and she always got my back."

"I got your back, baby," Angie moaned. She reached down in between Ax's legs and grabbed his manhood. She stroked it slowly with her hand as she looked lustfully into his eyes.

"Actually, you got my dick, Amanda," Ax joked. He grabbed the back of her hair tightly and pulled her head back exposing her neck. "Can I really trust you? How do I know you're not trying to set me up?"

"If you don't trust me, Ax, then why have you been spending nights with me?" Amanda questioned. "If I wanted to do something to you, I would have been made my move when you come over drunk and high." Ax looked at her questionably.

"You seem to have all the answers, don't you?" Ax replied. "But I just want you to know that I will kill you myself with my bare hands if you cross me!"

"It never even crossed my mind, lover, so stop your whining and kiss me!" A smug smile appeared on Amanda's lips, and Ax found her arrogance so sexy. He leaned down and pressed his lips firmly against hers and slid his tongue inside of her mouth forcefully. He trailed kisses down her neck and led his tongue down to her erect nipple. He flickered it against her hard nub, and Angie shuttered from the wonderful feeling. She took two handfuls of his hair and moaned at the pleasure Ax was providing.

"Turn the shower off," Ax ordered. "I'm going to lean you against this sink and fuck the shit out of you!"

"And here I thought you were just going to suck my titties," she joked coyly. Angie reached behind the shower curtain and turned off the water. Ax grabbed her by the back of her hair again and pulled her against him.

"Do you feel how hard my dick is? I'm about to tear that pussy up!" Ax declared.

"Well stop all your talking, and get to work!" Angie ordered. Ax leaned her over the bathroom sink and stared at her through the mirror. He heard the recording on her phone earlier and knew that it was probably Cecil's duck ass on the phone. Ax felt that Angie had some type of motive for fucking with him, but he wasn't exactly sure of her angle. She'd never asked him for anything except dick, but she always asked questions about his family. She listened to all of his problems and offered constructive advice to try to help him. However, all bitches start off doing the right thing, but that doesn't mean that they can keep up the act.

Ax rubbed his throbbing erection against the crease of her moistness and shoved it in roughly. Angie placed her hand against the mirror and looked at Ax with an amused smirk on her face. She figured Ax was in his feelings about the call, but in true male fashion, he wouldn't admit it to her. She would allow him to get this shit off today because she was generous like that. However, his little nasal problem was going to be the one thing that she planned on using against him to get everything she wanted, and more!

CHAPTER SEVENTEEN

$\mathcal{B}$ig Lee was behind the bar waiting on customers while she waited for Lay to come fill in for Ew Baby. Lay had called to tell her mother that Ew Baby was really sick with the flu bug and needed to stay at home in the bed for a couple of days. Big Lee offered to come check on Ew Baby, but Lay was very insistent that she didn't want her mother to catch whatever it was that got Ew Baby sick. Normally, Big Lee would have been around the corner in an instant because she could smell a lie from a hundred-yard radius. However, she'd been so distracted with the Geechie and Cecil situation that she didn't give it a second thought.

Big Lee came from around the counter and sat down at her spot at the bar. KeKe had come off her break so Big Lee could go back to watching the monitors and the customers. The front door opened and in comes Amber, with her long mink coat, expensive handbag, and red bottom shoes. Big Lee looked at her unimpressed and wondered why she had come to the lounge.

"Where is Jamal?" Amber demanded. Big Lee looked at her with a frown on her face.

"He ain't here, so you can carry yo' ass on back out the door!" Big

Lee hissed.

"I know your fat ass knows where the fuck he's at," Amber spat back. "You always seem to know where the fuck he is, and I would swear to God that he's attached to your ass by the hip!" Big Lee looked around patting her body all over. She got up from the stool and looked behind herself dramatically because she was amused by Amber's rhetoric.

"Nope! You're wrong about that, but he was attached to my pussy a few hours ago!" Amber looked at Big Lee and turned up her nose. "Bitch, you've got me sadly mistaken! It's not my fault that Whisper prefers the comforts of me instead of you! He never told you that he has a Big Lee fetish, and a skinny, broke bitch like you would never be able to satisfy him?" Big Lee scoffed. "And for the record, I'm not his fucking keeper! Call his phone like everyone else, and if he don't answer that means he doesn't want to talk to your ass!"

"Why don't you call him for me because I know he'll answer for you! We both know the only reason why Whisper even bothers with you, and your size has nothing to do with it!" Amber seethed, rolling her eyes.

"Ewww weee..." KeKe uttered. "That bitch is feeling brave today, Big Lee!"

"Ain't she?" Big Lee replied amused. "We gone see how tuff she is when I snatch her little narrow ass and slap the shit out of her!" Amber looked at Big Lee a bit nervously, but quickly gained her composure because she had one thing to defend herself with.

"You'll do nothing of the sort! I'm pregnant with Whisper's baby, and he'll be pretty upset if he finds out you put your hands on me!"

Amber protested.

"Bitch, you ain't pregnant and the lie you tell will blow up in your face! I'm the only bitch around here with a child by Whisper, and our baby is twenty-two years old!" Big Lee retorted. Amber looked at her strangely.

"You don't have a kid with Jamal," Amber argued. "Lay is his goddaughter, and you must be desperate if you're trying to pawn your daughter off on him."

"I don't have to do shit, because the truth don't need no proof!" Big Lee gloated. "We just sent off the DNA test last week, and the results should be back soon. I know what the results are going to be, but at least I have a real child against the figment of your imagination. See bitches like you are easy to read, and I guess you figured you could tell Whisper that you're pregnant in hopes that he'll be gullible enough to keep fucking you until you do get pregnant."

"I don't know what you're talking about, Big Lee," Amber insisted. "I know you've never liked me, and the feeling is definitely mutual! You're the reason why I can't get close to Jamal!"

"Correction, you're the reason why you can't get close to Jamal," Big Lee replied. "He sees that you're phony as a three-dollar bill, and all you want is his money. It's not my fault that your ass is transparent." Big Lee picked up her bottle of water and took a drink. "Why don't you do all of us a favor and get the fuck on some where! Whisper don't want you, and I've been sparing your ass for a while, but your luck has just about run out!"

"Are you threatening mme, Lee Ann?" Amber asked sarcastically.

She put her hand up on her hips and tried to act tough. On the inside she was shaking like a leaf, but she figured Big Lee wouldn't do anything to her, because in her mind, Jamal would be pissed.

"I don't make threats and, you should know that by now," Big Lee offered.

"I didn't think so," Amber gloated. Big Lee lifted one of her eyebrows and grabbed a cigarette out of her pack. She fired it up and took a big puff then blew the smoke in Amber's face. Amber waved her hand in front of her nose and coughed as the smoke shrouded her face.

"Are you trying to kill my unborn child?" Amber shuttered. "I'm sure Jamal is going to be outraged!"

"Bitch, you can kill the act. We both know that Whisper cut your ass loose a few months ago, and you must don't have any money, that's why you're coming around with this bogus pregnancy act."

"I am pregnant!" Amber insisted. "But for some reason, you don't want to accept it! I plan on having this child and whether you like it or not, Jamal is going to be a part of this baby's life… Unless you're willing to pay for me to disappear." Amber looked at Big Lee smugly and sat down on the bar stool next to her. "I know that you've been fucking Jamal behind my back, and he sneaks over to your house through the back. Also, I know that you're married to Cecil, and I'm sure he would be interested in knowing that his wife is fucking her chauffer." Amber had a shit-eating grin on her face, and she felt like she had the upper hand in the situation. What woman wouldn't want to hide the fact that they're having an affair, and from what Amber has heard about Cecil, this is something that Big Lee wouldn't want out in the open. "If you give me a half a million dollars, I would disappear; never to be seen again." Big Lee took a hit of her cigarette and thumped the ashes in a cup.

"You know I can make you disappear without even paying you the money." Big Lee looked at her smugly and blew the smoke out of her mouth. "I don't take kindly to threats, and my husband already knows that Whisper is my man. Also, Cecil knows that Layloni is Whisper's daughter too, so your words would fall on deaf ears, and you'll be the one stuck looking stupid." Amber didn't know what to say, because Big Lee had her card. She figured she could threaten Big Lee with telling Cecil, but it didn't matter because he already knew.

"Look, Lee Ann, I know that there's some type of arrangement we can make," Amber offered. "You know that Jamal is sweet for me, and I can convince him that being with me and the baby is the best thing for our family."

"But you ain't pregnant!" Big Lee insisted. "And if you keep telling that bold face lie, I'm going to make sure your ass falls off the face of the earth!" Amber's eyes bucked with nervousness because apparently, she couldn't talk her way out of this predicament.

"I'm not about to sit here and continue to take this shit!" Amber declared.

"Well get the fuck out! I didn't tell your stupid ass to come in here no way," Big Lee retorted. "And let me give you some valuable advice. Get the fuck out of dodge, because Jamal don't want that ass no more! We've been making it known to everyone that we're a couple now, and if you don't want to get your ass beat, stop coming around here spreading pregnancy rumors. It makes you look like a desperate bitch!" Amber jumped up from her stool with outrage. This was the reason why Jamal had broken up with her, and he would pay for that fatal mistake!

Lay walked into the lounge and noticed Amber standing next to her mother. It looked like they were in a heated exchange, but Lay knew that her mother would handle the situation. She walked over to the bar and put her purse down on the counter. She continued to watch the excitement between Amber and Big Lee because she knew that at any second, Amber would be getting up off the floor.

"I'm not about to sit here and keep going back and forth with you, Amber," Big Lee insisted. "Just get the fuck out of my lounge and keep calling Whisper!"

"I don't have to do sh---" Big Lee jumped up off her stool and grabbed Amber by her long hair weave. She pulled Amber's face down toward the floor and guided her straight to the door. You could hear Amber's heels click clacking against the floor hurriedly. Lay ran over and opened it up because she knew what her mother was about to do. Big Lee gave Amber one big shove, and she went flying backward onto the sidewalk.

"Damn, Ann! You throwing bitches out already?" Deacon questioned, walking up. He looked down at the ground and noticed it was Amber lying there. "Well damn, Amber! What the fuck have you done to be getting thrown out?"

"Fat bitch! You're going to pay for this! I'm pregnant and I'm going to press charges for assault!" Big Lee pulled her cellphone out of her pocket.

"I can call them right now," said Big Lee, pressing her code into the phone. Amber was shook, because that was the last thing she wanted to happen. If Big Lee called the police and she pretended to be pregnant, it would cause all types of problems and she would be facing a charge for making a fake report.

"Fuck you, Lee Ann!" Amber shouted. "And fuck Jamal, too! If he wants to be a part of his baby's life, then he knows how to find me!" Deacon reached down and helped Amber up off the ground. Big Lee looked at Amber and spat at her feet, then turned and went back into the lounge.

"Are you okay, pretty lady?" Deacon smiled. "Do you need me to drop you somewhere since Whisper is nowhere around?" Amber looked around for a second because she didn't have a ride. She had someone drop her off in hopes that Jamal would be at the lounge.

"As a matter of fact, I do need a ride, Deacon. Can you drop me off at a friend's house?" she asked coyly. Amber had heard stories from Whisper about Deacon being a sucker for slim women. Also, she remembered that Whisper said that Deacon was a trick and maybe she could con him out of a few dollars.

"I sure can, pretty lady," Deacon replied. "My car is this way."

CHAPTER EIGHTEEN

*E*w Baby had been hemmed up in the house for the past week and it was driving her crazy! She had to miss school due to the bruising on her face, and she almost had a close encounter with Big Lee the other day. She had missed two days of work, and Big Lee had become concerned about her daughter. She still needed to talk with her about Cecil, but there never seemed to be the right time. Lay had gone to school, and she made sure that breakfast was made for her sister. Lay had been taking good care of Ew Baby, and she insisted that if she was going to hang out with Byrd, it had to be done at their house. Byrd thought Lay was over-exaggerating about the damage ManMan had done to Ew Baby's face until he saw it for himself. He couldn't believe that ManMan had taken things that far, and he knew that once Big Lee got wind of what happened, she was going to send the goons for his ass.

Ew Baby figured that she could sneak out and run to the gas station without being spotted by anyone. She put a part down the middle of her hair and combed it down to cover her cheeks. She grabbed a baseball cap and a pair of dark shades to help camouflage and cover her face. Also, she put her hoodie on up under her coat and pulled the hood part up over the cap. This was even better because you could barely see her face at all.

Ew Baby walked out of the door and headed toward her car. She hit the chirp and was almost at the door when Ax pulled up on her and blew the horn obnoxiously. She looked over at him and grabbed the door because he was the last person she wanted to see her face. Ax blew his horn again and smiled at her, but when Ew Baby jumped in the car, it completely pissed him off. Ew Baby started up the engine while Ax jumped out and ran up to her door. He grabbed the handle and pulled it open forcefully, then stuck his head inside with a scowl on his face.

"What the fuck is up with you?" Ax snapped. "I've been calling your muthafuckin ass for the past week, and you've been sending my shit straight to voicemail! You know I don't like to be ignored, and it's taking all I have in me not to fuck you up!" Ew Baby sat paralyzed while Ax ranted and raved. "If you're feeling some type of way about me wanting you to be mine then all you have to do is tell a nigga! I love you, Ew Baby, and I'm tired of hiding my feelings!" Ax looked at Ew Baby as tears streamed down her cheeks. He wasn't sure if she was scared of what he had done or if she really thought he was going to beat her up, but whatever it was, Ax wanted to make it all right. "I'm sorry, Ew Baby," he uttered. He pulled her glasses off of her face and saw the bruising around her eye. He crushed her sunglasses in his hand before he snatched her up out of the car.

"Ax, please don't be mad at me!" Ew Baby begged. "I know I should have called you, but I was afraid of ---"

"You was afraid of what, Ew Baby?" Ax retorted. "What the fuck happened to your face?" Ew Baby wiped the tears from her eyes and lowered them.

"You hear me talking to you! Who did this to your face?" Ax thundered. The sound of his voice mad Ew Baby's heart stop for a split second, and she damn near fainted in his arms.

"Mmmmm… Mmmmm… ManMan did this to my face," Ew Baby stuttered. Ax's eyes widened, and a psychotic look came across his face. He snatched Ew Baby by the arm and drug her over to his car. He threw her in the passenger's seat, slammed the door, and walked around to the driver's side. He got inside and looked over at Ew Baby as he put his car in reverse. He hadn't shut the door before he backed back down the street, and cut the wheel causing the car to spin around in a half circle. He slammed on brakes and the door swung shut, then he threw the car in gear and shot up the street toward MLK.

"My car, Ax!" Ew Baby shouted.

"Fuck that car!" Ax hissed. "I'm about to go kill this nigga!" Ew Baby saw the look in his eye and knew that Ax wasn't playing. Luckily, Lay was coming down the street, and she noticed how crazy her uncle was driving. She saw that Ew Baby's car door was wide open and apparently it was running because smoke was coming from the exhaust. Lay figured Ax must have seen Ew Baby's face, so she knew exactly where they were headed.

Ax turned on McMillan and pulled up at the gambling house. He didn't see ManMan's car, so he figured the nigga was probably somewhere on the block. He pulled off with his tires screeching, and he headed down the street toward Walton because that's probably where the lil' nigga was located. Ew Baby texted Lay to tell her to call Big Lee. Ew Baby wanted ManMan to get his for what he'd done to her face, but she didn't want Ax to do anything to him in front of a lot of witnesses.

"Ax, please calm down," Ew Baby begged. "You know there's going to be a lot of people out, so I don't want you to jump out and do anything too stupid."

"Are you fucking serious, Ew Baby?" Ax shouted. "I'm sure your face was worse than this when it first occurred, wasn't it!" Ew Baby looked at him pitifully. "Wasn't it?" Ew Baby jumped from the intensity in his voice because she'd been around him before when he was this pissed off like this, and let's just say, it wasn't pretty. "So you sympathizing and taking up for this nigga, huh?"

"No, Ax!" Ew Baby assured him. "But I know your temper, and you'll jump out and kill him on the spot!" Ax looked over at Ew Baby and smirked then spotted ManMan's truck on the corner of McMillan and Walton. He gunned his Camaro down the street and turned the corner; damn near on two wheels. He pulled up in the middle of the street and threw his car in park. He jumped out and walked up on ManMan's truck and grabbed the door to open it. ManMan tried to hit the locks, but Ax was way too fast for him. He pulled it open and stared at ManMan with an evil grimace on his face before he snatched him by the collar and pulled him up out of the there.

"You put your hands on my gal?" Ax shouted angrily.

"I don't know what you're talking about, Ax!" ManMan whined. "I ain't touched your gal! Who the fuck is your gal?" ManMan asked with a perplexed look on his face.

"Ew Baby is my bitch, and she's been hiding from me because she didn't want me to see what the fuck you had done to her face!" Ew Baby got out of the car and walked over to the two men.

"Bitch ass nigga, you know you did this to my face! The nigga got mad because I called him a bitch ass nigga, and he grabbed me by the hair and punched me!" Ew Baby explained. "Now say I'm lying!"

"I...I...I... I did hit her, Ax, but look what the fuck she did to my face!" ManMan retorted. He pointed to where she'd dug her fingernails into his skin, and there were four perfectly spaced scratches on his right cheek. "The crazy bitch jumped out of the truck while it was rolling. I swear I didn't push her ass out!" Lay pulled up on the block and parked her car. She jumped out and popped her trunk, because ManMan was about to pay for what he'd done to Ew Baby.

"Fuck this weak ass nigga!" Lay shouted before she swung an iron baseball bat and hit ManMan in the knee. A surge of pain shot through his leg before his knee gave way, and he went crashing down on the pavement. Lay swung the bat and hit him a few more times against his leg, and Ew Baby ran up and kicked him in the stomach. She punched him a few times in the face and made sure that she blacked his eye like he'd done her. The two women were going crazy on ManMan when Byrd pulled up to see what was going on. He noticed Lay out there wildin' out, so he jumped out of the car and ran over to get her. He pushed through a crowd of people trying to get to her, but it seemed like there was no way that he could. He finally made his way to the front and tried to go grab Lay, when Whisper put his hand on Byrd's shoulder and stopped him in his tracks.

"You ain't got shit to do with this, young blood, so stay the fuck back!" Whisper ordered. Byrd looked at Whisper smugly.

"With all due respect, Whisper, I need to go stop my gal," Byrd informed him. "Lay shouldn't be out here fighting no nigga, and I don't want her to get hurt!"

"So you're trying to say that I'm going to let my daughter get hurt?" Whisper questioned. "I'd dead every nigga out here if I thought my baby was in danger!"

"I know, Whisper, but I just don't want her out her like this," Byrd insisted. "She's a fucking lady, my queen, and I'd be less of a man if I allowed this shit to continue!" Whisper looked at Byrd and saw the conviction in his eyes. He understood where Byrd was coming from, but he understood where Lay was coming from as well. "Please let me go get my baby, Whisper. I promise I won't let anything happen to her!" Whisper stared at Byrd for a moment then let him go. Byrd ran up on Lay and grabbed the bat before she could hit ManMan again. He was bloody and bruised up and would probably need stitches. The women put a beating on him that he'd never forget, and every other nigga would think twice before stepping to Ew Baby again.

"Come on, Lay!" Byrd spat, pissed. "You've done enough damage, and he'll probably need to go to the hospital."

"I don't give a fuck!" Lay retorted vehemently. "That nigga deserved the ass whooping we just gave him, and I bet he'll think twice before he puts his hands on another bitch!"

"You need to calm the fuck down, Lay, for real!" Byrd demanded. "You're out here like a got damn lunatic, and what would you have done if the police pulled up?" Lay looked at him smugly and turned up her nose.

"I'd go to jail and do the twenty hours on my head," Lay replied arrogantly. "My bond would be posted before I walked through the door of the station, and my mama would be down there to pick me up as soon as I was released!"

"You're impossible!" Byrd seethed. "That's besides the point, Lay, I was going to take care of this for you."

"But I didn't need for you to take care of this for me," Lay shot back. "That's not what I need you to do, Byrd… take care of things for me! I'm a grown ass woman that knows how to take care of myself! My mama, daddy, sister, and uncles got my back!"

"So you're ultimately saying fuck me, right?" Byrd questioned. Lay was so amped up on adrenaline that she wasn't thinking rationally. She didn't want to argue with Byrd, but she wanted him to understand that she didn't need him to fight her battles.

"That's not what I'm saying, Byrd, so don't put words in my mouth!" Lay scoffed. "I just want you to understand that I'm a capable body, and I'm used to handling my own shit! This wasn't your battle to fight, and we handled it on our own!" Byrd looked at Lay angrily because she was as stubborn as a mule. Byrd had watched Big Lee handle a many of niggas with her brothers, so he knew that Lay had that fighting spirit in her. "You mad?" Lay questioned as she folded her arms defensively in front of her body. She turned her lips up and cocked her head to the side. Byrd stared at her with a frown on his face, but his dick got hard from the cockiness his bitch was displaying. He loved Lay's smart mouthed ass, but he wasn't going to tolerate it. She was going to have to learn her place, and he was going to make sure that it happened; sooner rather than later!

Byrd stood in front of Lay and looked down at her sternly. His brow was furrowed as he narrowed his eyes at her. He was sizing his bae up because she was showing her ass, and Big Lee noticed what was going on as she watched intently from a distance.

"Is that nigga over there sizing up my baby girl?" Whisper snapped. He took a few steps, but Big Lee grabbed his arm firmly.

"You leave them alone, Whisper," Big Lee ordered. "They're working out their relationship, and they don't need your ass interfering!" Whisper glared at Big Lee, pissed.

"It looks like that nigga is trying to swell up on my baby!" Whisper argued.

"What that nigga's over there doing is the same thing you used to do to me when we were their age," Big Lee informed him. "Don't no real man want their gal out her fighting, and Byrd is chastising Lay for her actions."

"So you're condoning this shit?" Whisper questioned. "Fuck that!" He turned to go over to the couple when Lay wrapped her arms around Byrd's neck and hugged him. They shared a small kiss, and he slapped Lay on the ass. Next, Byrd put the bat up on his shoulder, and they strolled off to their cars with Lay's hand inside of his. Big Lee looked at her boo smugly and laughed all the way to the car.

CHAPTER NINETEEN

"*Y*ou really don't have to walk me into the house," Ew Baby uttered nervously. "I appreciate you snatching ManMan up for me, but I think I got things from here." Ax stood behind her on the steps, looking up at the back of her head. She put her key into the lock and Ax held the screen door open for her.

"Maybe I want to hang out with you because I miss your big head butt," Ax replied. "But if you don't want me here, then I'll leave."

"Oh no! You don't have to go," Ew Baby replied quickly. "I just figured you had something to do."

"I do," he replied sarcastically. "I'm coming in the house with you!" Ew Baby looked at him and smiled, and Ax winked his eye at her. They walked into the house and butterflies floated in Ew Baby's stomach. She'd heard what Ax had told ManMan, and she wondered how true his words were. Ew Baby wanted to ask him for clarification, but she was afraid of what he might say.

"You got something to drink?" asked Ax, taking off his leather jacket. "A nigga could sure use a hot cup of tea around this muthafucka."

"I don't have shit to make a long island, but---"

"I'm talking about regular tea, silly girl," Ax replied and laughed.

"I know y'all got that shit in here. Y'all lived with Big Lee, and she always kept a box of tea in her cabinet." Ew Baby laughed as she headed to the kitchen. She had taken off her coat and placed it on the coat rack.

"Hang your jacket up on the rack because I don't want to hear Lay's mouth when she comes into the house."

"She sounds like her mother," Ax joked.

"She's just like mama," Ew Baby uttered sarcastically. "She even tried to hide her relationship with Byrd like Mama did with Whisper." Ew Baby walked over to the sink with a teakettle and started filling it up with water. "I guess secret relationships are a thing with this family." Both Ew Baby and Ax laughed at the comment.

"Don't be talking about us like that," said Ax, walking up behind Ew Baby. "We have a secret relationship, so I guess you're just as guilty as them." He moved her hair over to the side then kissed Ew Baby on the nape of her neck. She tilted her head over to the side to welcome more kisses and a smile spread across her face with satisfaction.

"Did you mean what you said about me being your bitch?" Ew Baby shuttered as Ax brought his hands up her body and cupped her breast.

"You are my bitch, and I'm tired of hiding it from everyone," Ax confessed. He pressed his erection against her ass, and he continued to pinch and pull at her nipples.

"I've wanted you for a long time," Ew Baby confessed. "And if you want me then I'm yours." She pushed her ass back and wiggled it against his hard on, and he grabbed her tightly around the neck.

"Do you know what this means?" asked Ax, applying a little

pressure. Ew Baby gasped and almost came all over herself.

"Yes," she replied breathlessly. "You can have all of me, and I promise I'll be loyal to you!"

"You better be, Cecilia, because I'll kill you if you're not," Ax hissed. "You hold a lot of my secrets, Ew Baby, and I need you now more than ever." She grabbed his wrist and pulled his hand off her neck before she turned and stared in his eyes sincerely. She wanted him to understand that she was all his for the taking, and his words were music to her ears.

"You know I got you, Ax, and I love you with everything that I have in me," Ew Baby declared. "I've dreamed about this moment for so many years, but I envisioned it a little differently." Ax looked at her strangely.

"What do you mean?"

"I imagined that my hair and makeup would be flawless, and my outfit was a blue lace teddy because that's your favorite color," Ew Baby explained. "I've loved you since I was eight years old and you were eleven!" Ax looked down at Ew Baby and smiled as he cupped both of his hands on her cheeks. He looked into her eyes deeply, then leaned down and kissed her lips tenderly. Ew Baby opened her mouth and welcomed Ax's tongue as they continued to kiss passionately.

"Oh shit!" shouted Lay, covering her mouth. Byrd walked up behind her, and his mouth dropped open when he saw Ax and Ew Baby over at the sink making out. "What the fuck is going on?" Lay yelled frantically. "Why are y'all in here kissing?" Ax stared at Ew Baby and smiled before he turned to face his niece.

"It's really none of your business, niece, but since you seem so flustered by it, I guess I'll let you in," Ax replied sarcastically. "Ew Baby is my gal now, and we've been messing around for a while." Lay looked at Ew Baby smugly.

"Bitch! Why you ain't bothered to tell me?" Lay asked smugly. "I tell you everything, and you've been holding out on me!" Ew Baby looked at Lay shyly and smiled.

"We haven't been messing around like that," Ew Baby scoffed. "There's always been some sexual tension between us, but neither one of us acted on it until recently."

"Have y'all fucked?" Lay asked flat out. Ew Baby looked at Lay in disbelief.

"Damn, niece!" Ax called out and laughed. "I'm going to stop your line of questioning right there, and Ew Baby can answer that shit when I'm not around." Lay looked at both of them questionably.

"I don't have anything against it, and I want to go on record that I told you that my uncle liked you, bitch!" Lay hissed. A big smile spread across her face, and she held up the bag she was carrying. "We brought some Chinese food from around the corner, and there's enough for all of us!" Byrd held up the two bags he was carrying and smiled at Ax.

"Thanks for the offer, but maybe we'll eat some later," Ax replied. Lay looked at him strangely.

"Can I at least have a spring roll?" Ew Baby whined.

"How do you know that she has spring rolls?" Ax questioned.

"Because Lay always buys spring rolls when she gets Chinese

food." Ew Baby shrugged her shoulders and walked toward the table. "Why can't we eat anyway?" Ax wiggled his eyebrows at her.

"I really don't want to talk like this around my niece, but I want to go fuck you," Ax explained. "And since we're in a sharing mood; for the record, we've never fucked, Lay. This will be the first time, so don't mind all the moaning, groaning, and screaming you're about to hear." Lay looked at her uncle smugly.

"I think we're about to take our food and go over Byrd's house," Lay uttered. "I don't think I can handle it!" Everyone laughed because Lay was being dramatic. "What the fuck is Mama going to say when she finds out?" Ew Baby bit into her spring roll and looked at Lay, confidently.

"Mama and I had a talk about it, and she gave me her blessing," Ew Baby explained. "She said that she could see the way that Ax looks at me, and it was evident that he wanted to fuck."

"Did my big sis really say that?" Ax asked curiously.

"Those weren't her exact words, but she knew that you wanted me." A satisfying grin came across Ax's face, while Lay and Byrd watched both Ax and Ew Baby intently. "Okay, I'm ready!"

Ew Baby and Ax went up to her room while Lay and Byrd settled in the living room to watch a movie and eat their food. Ew Baby was so nervous about being with Ax for the first time that her palms and underarms were sweating. She nervously wandered around her room, and Ax was on her heels everywhere she moved.

"Do I make you nervous?" Ax asked seductively.

"A little bit," Ew Baby admitted anxiously. "But I need to take a shower."

"Maybe I want that pussy a little bit funky," Ax teased as he grabbed and pulled Ew Baby into him. He pressed his lips firmly against hers, and he thrust his tongue inside of her mouth. He could feel Ew Baby's body slightly trembling, and his stomach sunk in with butterflies. This was the first time that he'd felt nervous about going up inside of some pussy, and the feeling frightened him. He pulled away from Ew Baby and stared into her eyes. "Would you be disappointed if I didn't want to fuck?" Ew Baby looked at him with a distraught look on her face.

"Did I do something wrong? Is it because I'm ugly," she cried. "I knew that this was too good to be true!"

"Stop talking crazy, girl," Ax demanded. "I don't give a fuck about your face being fucked up! That shit means nothing to me!"

"So why you don't want to have sex with me?" she questioned. She reached her hand down inside of Ax's grey jogging pants, and she wrapped her hand around the shaft of his rod. "Ohhhh… you're so thick," she moaned, licking her lips seductively. Ax stared into her eyes as his member stiffened against her hand.

"I told you," he replied arrogantly. "But now that I think about it, I want our first time to be special."

"Ahhh… Is Axel Wilson a romantic man?" Ew Baby teased. He pulled her hand out his pants and pulled her over to the bed. He sat down on it and pulled Ew Baby on his lap.

"You mean more to me than you know, Cecilia," Ax admitted. "You've been riding with me ever since you were fourteen years old and not once have I heard anyone say some shit that they shouldn't know. You've been with me when I've killed niggas. You've helped me hide evidence and even held me all night when Killa Cam died." Ew Baby saw the innocence in his eyes as he poured his heart out to her. "You've shown me that you're the one for me, but I want you to understand that it's not going to be easy being my woman." Ew Baby stoked his face and kissed his lips softly.

"I know," she whispered before she kissed his lips again. She pressed hard this time and tilted her head to the side. Ax gripped her tightly as their tongues danced in and out of each other's mouths. He pulled away from Ew Baby and stared at her for a moment.

"Look, Ew Baby, there are some things that I need to explain to you," Ax informed her. "We have a lot of things to talk about, and all I want to do is cuddle…" he kissed her lips softly. "Rub this little onion shaped ass of yours and bare my soul to you." He kissed her again, but this time nastily. He sucked on her bottom lip and her insides melted like ice cream. "Can you handle that?"

"I think so," she whispered as Ax rubbed his hands against her thighs. "But you're going to have to stop rubbing me like that if you don't plan on fucking me." Ax smiled and kissed her lips once more. He pressed his forehead against hers and rubbed her cheek with his hand. He was about to tell Ew Baby about the demons that haunted his dreams at night, and she was very receptive to his madness.

CHAPTER TWENTY

*C*ecil was headed to the visitor's room feeling a bit confused. Angie didn't mention that she was coming to see him, and he knew it definitely wasn't Big Lee waiting for him. There were a million thoughts going through his head, and when he walked into the room, an evil scowl came across his face instantly. He gave the CO his badge then walked over to the table where Geechie was waiting. Cecil wanted to wrap his hands around his brother's neck, but he didn't want to do anything to jeopardize his out date. He had one more month before he was to be released from prison, and he didn't need anything to interfere with his freedom.

"What the fuck is you doing here?" Cecil huffed angrily. "I thought I told you to get out of Missouri and go lay low in Chicago."

"It's good to see you too, brother," Geechie scoffed. "I came to talk to you because I had to get out of Chicago. Apparently, Big Lee has family down there, and I almost got pinched a few times because she pays well for information." Cecil continued to stare at his brother disapprovingly, but he sat down at the table across from Geechie.

"And what the fuck you want me to do about it?" Cecil hissed. "You fucked up things between Big Lee and I, so I'm going to have to figure out another way to get what I need when I get out of prison!"

"That bitch Angie has been making major moves," Geechie complained. "Did you know that she was fucking Ax?" Cecil looked at his brother smugly.

"Yeah, I know she's fucking Ax," Cecil replied annoyed. "I'm the one who told her to get on the nigga. I had heard some shit about him around the yard, and I figured she would be able to pull him."

"Well she in fact did that shit, but did you know that they're quite an item. A few of my guys said that he's been parading her around like the homecoming queen," Geechie mentioned smugly. "I think the bitch is in love with the nigga because I overheard them on the phone together, and she was all lovey dovey and shit!"

"How did you hear their conversation?" Cecil asked curiously. "I told you to stay away from her!"

"Calm your ass down!" Geechie hissed. "I stopped by there to get a few things that I had left behind at her house. I looked through the window to see if she had company, and she was sitting on the couch talking to him on the phone." Cecil looked at him skeptically, but there could be some truth to it. "She was playing with her pussy, and I think they were having phone sex!"

"Nigga, she was talking to me!" Cecil shouted in frustration. The guard looked at him sternly, and Cecil threw his hands in the air. "My fault, CO!" Geechie looked around the room then focused his attention back on Cecil.

"Look, Cecil," said Geechie looking around nervously. "I gotta get some money, and quick! I ain't been able to make no moves, and

I'm down to my last couple of hundred dollars."

"That ain't my problem, lil' brother," Cecil said nonchalantly. "You fucked up both of our bread and butter, so you're going to have to figure some shit out."

"That's the wrong answer, Cecil!" Geechie retorted. "You better figure some shit out or else I'm gonna have ta put the word out that you like to play them back door games." Geechie looked around the room and spotted a nigga he knew from the Ville. He and the female that was visiting him kept staring over at their table, so Geechie knew that word was going to get back to Big Lee. "I gotta few comrades behind these walls, and they told me that you and your celly are *real familiar*; if you know what I mean." Cecil's face drew up into a scowl, and he squeezed his fist tightly together.

"Muthafuckas are telling tall tales, so whatever you heard is a got damn lie!" Cecil replied adamantly. "I ain't fucking no nigga, and whoever told you that got me completely fucked up!"

"They didn't say you were fucking a man..." Geechie seethed smugly. "They said you liked to get fucked!" Cecil jumped up from his seat and stared at Geechie angrily.

"This fucking visit is over 'cause you got me fucked up!" Cecil shouted.

"Inmate! Your visit is terminated," the CO shouted from his desk.

"No problem, CO! This muthafucka was over anyway!" Cecil retorted, staring at Geechie angrily.

****

Geechie couldn't believe that Cecil flipped out on him like that at the visit. He was driving down Highway 70 on his way back to St. Louis because that bitch Angie was about to come off some money. Geechie wasn't going to rob her but strong-arm her instead. He knew that Cecil would get over himself and see that he would truly be fucked up if he stayed mad at him. Geechie needed some money real bad, and somebody was going to have come on home with some paper. He was deep in thought when his phone went off breaking his concentration. He quickly grabbed it out of the cup holder and examined the unknown number on the screen.

"State yo' peace," Geechie spat into the phone.

"What's the word, moe?"

"Shit! Who the fuck is this?" Geechie retorted.

"So you don't know my voice, Geechie! Damn nigga, has it been that long?"

"If you don't state yo' fuckin' name, I'm goin' hang the fuck up on you!"

"That's fucked up, Geechie! This—" Geechie hung up the phone and threw it back in the cup holder. It started to go off again, and Geechie just looked at it angrily. The phone stopped ringing for a second then started to go off again. Geechie grabbed it up and hit the answer button. "Don't hang up, Geechie, this Booker! This Booker, bruh!"

"I was about to go off on your ass, nigga! I told you to state yo' name and you want to stroll down memory lane!" Geechie complained. "What the fuck you want?"

"I heard you was running from Big Lee and her brothers, but I got a lick and I need someone with your expertise to help me pull it off," Booker explained.

"Booker, I ain't getting into none of your lame brain schemes! The last time I did some shit with you. I almost got my ass locked up!" Geechie hissed angrily.

"I promise you, Geechie! This shit is butter!" Booker assured him. "A muthafucka reached out to me and asked if I would do him a solid. I didn't trust the nigga at first, because we don't get down like that for real. He needed this handled outside his circle, and he knew that I was wit' robbing a muthafucka. All we have to do is wait for a muthafucka to come make a drop off and jump out on his ass. It's going to be like taking candy from a baby!" Geechie stared at the traffic ahead of him and scratched his chin instinctively.

"Where you at?" Geechie asked as he picked up a cigarette out of the pack, lying on the console.

"I'm on the north side," Booker replied. "Call me when you get to Salamas Market downtown, and I'll come meet you on the parking lot."

"Bet," Geechie agreed then hung up the phone. He had no problem robbing a nigga out of some dope. He could take that shit and sale some of it to make some money, and tuck some away to tweak his nose. It was a win, win situation all the way around. Geechie thanked God for this blessing that fell into his lap, but he had to secure a place to stay before he made it back to St. Louis.

****

"Hey, Sweetie! I wasn't expecting a call from you until later on tonight," Angie beamed.

"I know, but that nigga Geechie came to visit me, and he pissed me the fuck off!" Cecil explained. "I'm gone need for you to tighten your shit up and be more careful how you move around."

"Why? What's wrong?" Angie asked nervously. "Did he say something to you about me? I know something's wrong, because I can hear it in your voice." Cecil held the phone for a few minutes without saying a word.

"Geechie has been watching you through your window," Cecil informed her. "I think he was there yesterday because he said something about hearing you having phone sex."

"We had phone sex yesterday, so that creep was being a peeping tom last night!" Angie fumed! "That means he saw my---"

"Angie, that shit ain't important!" Cecil hissed. "Geechie said that some niggas up in here told him that I was fucking around with your brother."

"Are you?" Angie asked inquisitively. "I found it interesting that he wanted to help you, and the only reason why he would do that is if he had a shared interest."

"Look! I don't know what the fuck you're implying, but I'm getting tired of muthafuckas saying that I'm gay!"

"I didn't say that, Cecil," Angie protested. "However, me and my brother have always been honest with one another. He doesn't hide shit from me, and when we first started this thing that we got going, he told me some things that I don't care to repeat."

"Whatever that nigga said he was lying!" Cecil insisted. "I... I... I... just needed some help because my wife turned her back on me!"

"That's not what my brother said, but I don't give a fuck, Cecil. Since I've been fucking with you, I've been able to save a lot more money unlike dealing with my brother. He's a little stingy, and he liked to use his money to control me. The truth of the matter is, Shine has fallen off, and helping you brought him back in the game. He spent most of his money on litigation, and we both had been living off of it for awhile," Angie explained.

"That muthafucka souped me up and used me!" Cecil uttered confused. "I can't believe I let him get in my head. I... I... I..."

"Look, Cecil, you're not the only person that Shine has tricked into his uhhh---"

"Into his what?" Cecil shouted. He noticed he was obviously too upset, which made him feel guilty of what everyone was implying. "Look, Angie, I gotta go!"

"Cecil, wait..." *Click!* Angie held the phone for a minute with a look of disbelief on her face. She jumped up off the couch and went over to her front window. She pulled up the blinds and canvased her yard. She'd better get her gun and keep it close because, if Geechie so much as looked at her wrong, Angie was going to plug his ass!

CHAPTER TWENTY-ONE

*B*yrd cupped Lay's ass as she rocked back and forth on his stiff erection. She cupped her breast and pinched her nipples because her man felt so good inside of her wetness. She leaned down and kissed Byrd's lips nastily, as he pushed himself further up inside of her.

"Oh bae… you feel so good," Lay moaned. She licked his lips then breathed heavily inside his mouth when he grabbed her breast and put one of her nipples in his mouth. She pressed her hands against the leather headboard and held her head backward as her orgasm rose up from her core. "I'm cummin'! Aaaahhhh…" Lay cried while Byrd continued sucking her clit, hard. She rocked back and forth, bouncing wildly as her orgasm took control of her. She collapsed on top of him, but Byrd wasn't finish, yet. He flipped Lay over on her back and dug himself deep inside of her womb. Lay gasped as the pressure from his dick hit the bottom of her pelvis and took a quick turn into her fallopian tube. Lay's eyes widened, and she put her hand against his chest. "Oh my God, Byrd Man! What the fuck is you doing to me?"

"You ain't never had a nigga touch the bottom before, baby?" Byrd groaned. He leaned down and kissed her lips firmly as he pumped inside of her rhythmically. They had Pandora playing over the Bose speaker, and the 90's Love Song station was jammin'. "I'm just practicing for that moment when you let a nigga put a baby up in this juicy muthafucka!" A smile spread across Lay's face, and she leaned up and kissed him lustfully. Byrd pushed Lay's legs up over his shoulders and went buck wild on the pussy. He was beating and pounding it up with brute force, and even though it was hurting Lay's inside, it still felt good to her. She placed her hand on Byrd's chest once more, and it helped brace the blows. He felt himself about to nut, so he released Lay's legs and cupped her ass tightly. He humped her like a Jackrabbit, and he shot his load inside of her. Byrd buried his face inside the nape of Lay's neck as he groaned and grunted. She raised her legs and wrapped them around his waist and squeezed his butt with both hands. Byrd looked up and smiled at his glowing girlfriend then fell on top of her feeling exhausted.

"You got a nigga straight in love," Byrd proclaimed. "If you ever give my pussy away, Lay, I swear before God I will fuck you up!" Lay laughed as she pushed him up off of her.

"Nigga, you're the one who instantly shook to another bitch, so don't you fuck up anymore, or I'm gone get yo' ass together!" She got up out of bed and headed to the bathroom. "Are you going to join me in the shower?" Byrd's phone went off and Lay stopped in mid stride. She looked over at him smugly then waited for him to answer.

"Hello." Byrd smiled at Lay because he could see that she had copped an attitude instantly.

"Hey Byrd, you busy?" ManMan asked dryly.

"A little," he replied. "What's up?" Lay crossed her arms in front of her and shifted her weight to one foot.

"Aye, I got this nigga over here at the trap that want a full-figured girl, and he has the money with him right now," ManMan explained.

"Did you count it?" Byrd asked, getting up off the bed. "I need to be sure that everything is there before I make this trip across town." Byrd was around the corner at Lay's house, but he didn't want ManMan to know that he was that close.

"Let me call you back, and I'll tell you what's up." Byrd hung up the phone and threw it on the bed before he stopped directly in front of Lay.

"Why are you standing here with an attitude, lil' girl?" Byrd questioned.

"I guess you're about to go make a run," she replied dryly. She cut her eyes at him and stuck her lips out.

"You know what I do for a living, Lay, and when money calls I have to answer. You know that," Byrd replied frankly. He put his hands on her hips and pulled her in closely. He turned his head and shook it at her in an antagonizing manner. "I'm getting close to my goal, and then I won't have to sell dope no more." Lay looked at him and laughed.

"Nigga, you're marrying me, and dope is what makes our world go 'round," Lay replied and laughed. She wrapped her arms around his neck and stared into his eyes lovingly. She knew that Byrd was driven, and he'd been hustling hard since Cam had died. There were many nights where she had to go to bed alone, but she knew that it would all pay off in the long run. "Who was that on the phone?"

"That was the home girl, Mara. She said a nigga came through talking about he wanted a brick, so I told her to make sure that the nigga had the money." His phone went off and they both looked over at it. Lay let out a long loud sigh, and she pushed away from Byrd.

"Go answer your phone, and I'm about to go get in the shower," she complained. Lay walked over to a chair that sat in the corner of her room and picked up her robe. She slipped it on and pouted the entire time, and Byrd found her display of discontentment cute.

"I'll be in there in a minute," Byrd replied, walking over to the bed. He picked his phone up and answered it as Lay walked out of the room. "What's the word?"

"It's all here," ManMan answered. "What you wanna do?" Byrd held the phone for a minute and stared at the bed. He wanted to go get in the shower then post up with Lay and watch television.

"You ain't got it?" Byrd asked curiously. "I don't feel like leaving the house, truthfully."

"You gone pass up all this paper for some pussy?" ManMan scoffed. "I'll never put a bitch before my money!"

"I ain't putting no bitch before my paper," Byrd hissed. "You got me fucked up!"

"Whatever, dude," ManMan replied. "Your girl and her hoe of a sister had done a number on me! I got a broken arm and three cracked ribs."

"I guess you'll think twice before you put your hands on another woman," Byrd uttered. Lay's phone dinged alerting her that she had a text message and Byrd looked over at it.

"Whatever, Byrd. You coming or not?" ManMan snapped.

"Nigga, you better watch your tone," Byrd hissed. "I wasn't the one who fucked you up, and if you know what's good for you, you'll leave this shit alone and call it even." ManMan held the phone for a second because he didn't know how to respond. He felt some type of way about the beat down, but he was grateful that Ax didn't kill him. "I don't think I'm coming out. Let me make a phone call and I'll hit you back in a minute."

Byrd hung up the phone and walked over to the nightstand on Lay's side of the bed. He looked down at her phone, and the text message she had received was sitting on the screen. He looked at the name then read the message, and an instant rage rose up inside of him. The message was from Reed, and it was apparent that Lay had been communicating with the nigga.

Text Message (Reed): I guess you were busy the other night that's why you didn't answer your phone. I've been trying to get in contact with you, but it seems like the shit with your uncle is really taking a toll on you, and I don't want you to shut me out! I love you, and I want you to come to Spain. Give it some thought and please call me! One

Byrd's eyes narrowed at the phone because why the fuck is some nigga texting his gal telling her that he loves her, and that he wants her to leave the country to come see him. Did Lay not tell that nigga that her soon to be husband has locked her ass down! Byrd wanted to know what the fuck was Lay's angle by not saying anything, because he thought they were passed her trying to hide their relationship.

"I took a shower without you," said Lay, walking into the room.

She noticed the angry look on his face, and she wondered what was going on. "What's wrong with you?"

"Why the fuck is this nigga texting you talking about he loves you, and wants you to come to Spain?" Byrd spat sternly.

"What are you talking about, and why are you searching through my phone?" Lay asked defensively. "Are you that insecure about us, Byrd?"

"I ain't insecure about shit!" Byrd huffed. "But I don't appreciate the fact that you ain't told this nigga that you belong to me!"

"Who is this nigga you keep referring to?" Lay asked throwing her hands up to her shoulders. "And again, why the fuck are you searching through my phone? I know bitches be on your phone all of the time, but you don't see me freaking out about it!"

"If a bitch on my phone then she's buying dope!" Byrd retorted. "I thought you said you wasn't feeling that nigga, Reed!" Lay was ready to respond but stopped when Byrd said Reed's name.

"Reed?" Lay uttered. "I told you that his feelings were a lot stronger than mine. I've been ignoring his ass, and that's probably why he's sending me a message."

"Naw, you've been talking to that nigga," Byrd insisted.

"No, I haven't!" Lay walked over to Byrd and attempted to pick her phone up off the nightstand. Byrd snatched it up before she could get it and punched in her code.

"What are you doing?" Lay shouted. She tried to get her phone from him, but he held his arm up in the air.

"I'm about to pull your messages up from this nigga, and we're about see if you're lying to me!" Byrd retorted. "And I swear to God, Lay, if you're lying to me, I'm going to make an exception and smack the shit out of you!"

"I thought you don't put your hands on women," Lay said angrily. "You're making a big deal out of nothing!"

"Am I really?" he replied. "Why you ain't tell this nigga that you're my gal? You should have told his ass that it was over and that you belong to me now!"

"Listen to you! You sound like a child," Lay scoffed. "I love you, Byrd and I'm not interested in no other man! However, if you think I'm trying to be sneaky and do shit behind your back, then maybe you should re-evaluate whether or not you want to be with me!" Byrd glared down at Lay because he was hotter than fish grease. It was apparent that Lay couldn't see his point, so he felt it was best to just leave.

"Aye, I'm about to go handle some business," Byrd uttered frankly.

"I don't think you should go," Lay replied. "We need to settle this shit because I ain't gone keep arguing with you about an irrelevant ass nigga!"

"Irrelevant, huh?" Byrd chuckled. "I bet he was going to be the go to nigga whenever your ass got mad at me. He sure popped up when all that other shit jumped off."

"That was a fluke, and even then, I wasn't feeling his ass," Lay replied. "I can't believe how insecure you're acting. You know I'm down for you, nigga, so quit acting like a bitch, and give me my phone!"

"So I'm a bitch now?" Byrd retorted. "I ain't never disrespected you or called you out of your name; not even when you stabbed me!" He looked at her crossly. "So you think I'm a bitch, Lay?" She stared at him nervously because of the enraged look on his face.

"I don't think you're a bitch, Byrd, and I'm sorry for saying that. I didn't tell Reed about us, because I haven't talked to him! I figured if I ignored him enough he would get the picture," Lay explained. "Should I have told him when he first contacted me after we made it official, yes. However, I ain't checking for that nigga 'cause it's all about you!" She walked up on him with puppy dog eyes and tried to ease things over. "You know it's all about you, Byrd. Why are you trying to make a big deal out of nothing?"

"It's the principle of the whole thing, Lay," Byrd replied and grabbed her up by her nightgown. He stared intently into her eyes with a hard frown on his face. "Don't you ever fix your mouth to call me a bitch again, or I swear for God, Lay, you're going to be sorry!" He pushed her down on the bed and walked over to his clothes. "I'm about to go make a move." Lay looked up at him feeling some type of way. A part of her wanted to jump up and swing on him, but the look on his face made her think twice about it.

"What do you mean you're about to go make a move?" Lay stammered.

"I told you that when money calls, I have to answer," he uttered, putting on his underwear.

"Are you coming back?" she asked wearily. He pulled up his pants and ignored Lay's question. He felt it was time that he quit being passive with Lay and her attitude. He figured any man that dealt with the Wilson women had to have thick skin because when you have women that possess a lot of power, they tend to forget how to respect men that they love due to it.

"Quit asking me all these muthafuckin' questions and wait the fuck here to see!"

CHAPTER TWENTY-TWO

*W*hisper was at home cleaning up after the crazy afternoon he'd just had. He received a fucked up message from Amber, and she said that Big Lee had threw her out of the lounge because she had come there searching for him. She had been blowing up his phone for the past month begging for money. She told him that her rent was overdue, and the landlord was threatening to put her out on the streets. She tried to use the fact that she was pregnant to appeal to his caring nature, but a conversation that he'd had with Amber's best friend revealed that she indeed wasn't pregnant, and it was a ploy to get money out of Whisper. His first thought was to go slap the shit out of Amber, but he figured Big Lee's actions today would have to be sufficient enough. Besides, he was getting tired of the way things were between him and Big Lee, and if she was going to be his woman, shit was definitely going to have to change!

Big Lee closed up early and decided to go home to cuddle up with Whisper. She hadn't seen him since earlier, and he always came to get her at night because he wanted to make sure that she made it home safely. Teke walked Big Lee to her car, and made sure that she pulled off safely, but it didn't feel right without Whisper being there. She didn't remember them getting into an argument or anything, so she couldn't understand why he hadn't come around at all this evening.

Big Lee pulled up in front of her house and noticed all of the lights were out. She got out of the car and looked down the street at Whisper's house. She noticed that the lights were on at his place, so the decision was made to where she would go. She shut her car door and pressed the key fob, trying to decide whether or not to click out on him. She figured Amber was up in there with him, and that's why he's been a ghost with her. However, a feeling came over her, and she reconsidered her approach. Big Lee felt like it was time for her to make some changes in the way that she treated Whisper. He didn't deserve to be punished for all of Cecil's bullshit, and after a long talk she had tonight with Deacon, it was apparent that Whisper was getting tired of the shit as well.

Big Lee put her keys in her pocket and headed toward her lover's house. She wanted to have a heart to heart talk with him, and decided tonight was the night for them to solidify the place that he would have in her life from here on out because, either she was going to drive him away or he was going to get tired of her slick ass mouth and attitude and leave her the fuck alone. She opened up the screen door and knocked twice. She held her breath until he opened the door, because her nerves were getting the best of her, and she hoped her voice didn't shake when she spoke. Whisper opened up the door and looked at her strangely.

"Hey, baby," said Big Lee with a pleasant smile on her face.

"Hey, baby," he replied. He looked outside and searched to see if anyone else was out there with her. "What you doing off so early? I was just about to walk down there to get you."

"I decided to close early, because it was slow," Big Lee replied. "Can I come inside or are you busy?"

"Don't say no dumb shit like that to me. Of course you can come inside," he replied moving out of the way. Big Lee walked into the house, and the smell of lemons and bleach clouded her nose intensely.

"It smells like you're cleaning up. Should I leave and come back?" Big Lee asked, turning to face him. She bumped into him awkwardly and placed her hands on his chest. She looked up at him stupidly and swallowed hard. "Excuse me," Big Lee uttered anxiously. Whisper looked at her and shook his head because he knew Ann was on one, and he hoped it didn't have anything to do with Amber's stupid ass.

"Now why would you want to do that?" Whisper asked curiously. "I had just finished up and was about to come down to the lounge; I just told you that." He placed his hands on her shoulders and kissed her lips tenderly. "Come on!" He grabbed her hands and wrapped his arms around her waist with her back pressed against his chest. He led them into the kitchen, and he kissed her once more on the cheek. "Are you hungry?"

"A little," she replied, taking off her coat. Whisper grabbed it from the back and helped her the rest of the way out of it. He left out the room for a second to put it in the closet. Big Lee looked around and noticed how clean and meticulous Whisper's kitchen was set up. He had everything organized and color coordinated. The gadgets that adorned the counter tops had Big Lee curious about the man she realized she knew so little about all of a sudden.

"What are you hungry for?" Whisper asked walking back into the kitchen.

"I just realized something, Whisper. We spend so much time together, but I really don't know certain personal things about you," Big Lee mentioned wearily.

"Things like what, Ann?" he asked curiously. "You know my birthdate. You know all of my family. You know my favorite drank, foods, color, and sports teams. What else is there for you to know?" Big Lee looked at Whisper warmly and smiled.

"I do know all of those things, but I want to know more about you. I want to know your hopes, your dreams, and fears. I think you know more about me than I do of you. Why is that?" she questioned. Whisper looked at her strangely and walked over to the sink. He turned on the water and washed his hands.

"Maybe it's because you were too consumed with your husband," Whisper replied. He grabbed a paper towel off of the holder and wiped his hands. He turned to face Big Lee and stared at her intently. "My hopes are that we can figure this thing out between us because I feel like more of an accessory to you, and it's starting to really bother me. My dream is that when the time was right, you'll become my wife, and we can be a real family with our daughter. My fear is that you're going to drive me away, because you have a tendency to emasculate me, and I don't like it! I've done a good job of hiding my feelings, but I'm tired of your brothers saying slick shit to me, and even Teke has started to get in on the shit, and I'm going to knock that nigga out!" Big Lee looked at

Whisper and smirked. "I mean… I know it's difficult to be a powerful woman, but you need to understand that it's difficult for a man to be by the side of one. Sometimes I feel like you get some type of satisfaction out of talking to me crazy, but then I remember that you grew up in a house full of niggas, and your mother didn't make it any better by the way she talked to your father." Big Lee looked at Whisper solemnly as he spoke to her. She didn't get upset, because these were some of the things that she'd already heard from Deacon. Deacon told her that she was going to lose Whisper if she didn't change her ways, and that was the last thing she wanted to happen.

"I want to apologize to you if I made you feel like less of a man. I think sometimes I do it unconsciously, but it still doesn't make it right," Big Lee acknowledged. "Growing up, I watched how my mother talked and treated my father. He was a strong man, but my mother's big personality tended to be what governed the household. She hated the relationship that I had with my father, because he treated me like a princess, and I got away with everything! She was the reason why I married Cecil, and I regret ever listening to her. I think part of the problem with me and my mother is that she always tried to control me, and I rebelled against it. She didn't like me messing with you, because of our age difference, but that shit never mattered to me. You was the one who came on to me, and it took a while for you to wear me down." They both laughed because Whisper knew that was the truth. He leaned back against the counter and crossed his arms in front of him. He was happy that they were having this conversation because he loved her just as much as she loved him. However, he wasn't going to keep taking this shit off of her. "It's fucked up that the one time I took my mother's advice was the worst mistake of my life, and I'm paying for it right now as we speak. If I would have listened to you and said fuck Cecil, Cam would still be alive today." Big Lee looked down at the counter for a second, and when she looked up, there were tears in her eyes. "Whisper, I love you… but I don't know how to. All I know how to do is be aggressive and not really express my feelings in a feminine manner. I had to go by the same rules as everyone else, and Mama never took the time to show me how to be a lady. What little I learned when I was younger came from my grandmothers', and that was only when I spent time with them."

"Ann, I know how you grew up," Whisper reminded her. "Remember I was right there with you. However, that has nothing to do with the way you talk to me. Do you know sometimes I want to call you a bitch, and I even felt like slapping the shit out of you a couple of times." Big Lee looked up at him in shock, but then her face softened a bit.

"I could see that," she admitted. "But I don't know what to do, Whisper, 'cause all I know how to do is get money and be a boss bitch. I have a staff of over a hundred people, and I have to keep them in line. If you let a nigga slide once, then they think they can ice skate!" Whisper wanted to laugh at her statement, but he was trying to be serious with her. He felt like if he let up and cracked a smile, she'd think she was in the clear.

"But you don't have to keep me in line, Ann. I don't want shit from you, but your love and respect! I have never asked you for shit, so you can't say that I'm with you for the money; even though we get that paper together, and maybe my behavior might have implied that because I've allowed you to talk to me or treat me like a little boy. However, that shit is about to change!" Whisper declared. "Because if you can't treat me with more respect and talk to me like I'm a grown ass man, then we don't need to continue any further with a romantic relationship and things can be strictly business. I'll just start fucking hoes and live the bachelor's life like Ax." Big Lee furrowed her brow, and wiped the tears from her eyes because she understood everything that Whisper was saying to her.

"You know I'm going to fall short sometimes," she uttered. "Can you help a sista out?"

"Truthfully, Ann, I can't help you. You're going to have to work on this yourself, but I will be supportive. I love you more than anything in this world, but I refuse to go another day with you treating me like less of a man." He walked over to Big Lee and wiped her tears away. Next, he leaned down and kissed her lips tenderly then pulled away and stared lovingly. "Now that we got that out of the way, what do you want to eat?" Big Lee let out a sigh of relief.

"Whatever you want to fix, baby," she replied and smiled.

****

Whisper and Big Lee had continued to talk while he prepared a dinner of shrimp and chicken alfredo pasta with salad and garlic bread on the side. They told each other their deepest secrets and shared their wants and needs from one another in their relationship. Big Lee had started going to a therapist once a week, and this was one of the things that he told her that she needed to do if she wanted to decrease her stress. She needed to positively express herself without going from zero to hundred at a blink of an eye. Also, she discovered that Whisper was her rock, and she needed him whether she wanted to admit it or not. Maybe God was working in her favor because, tonight was an eye opener for both of them, and hopefully they would be able to continue to build a stronger relationship with one another.

Whisper was watching television and Big Lee had just drifted off to sleep. They had an hour long sex session after dinner, and she was laid up on Whisper's chest with her leg thrown over his thigh. Big Lee was lying in the wet spot, but apparently she didn't mind, because she settled right on it without hesitation. She'd visited Whisper's house all of the time, but this was the first time that she'd spent the night. Normally, he would be afraid that Amber would show up, so it was best that they stayed at Big Lee's house. Plus, everyone always hung out at her house, so he was always there. It didn't make sense for them to leave to go to his house, so naturally they would stay there instead of leaving.

Whisper's phone started to ring, and he looked over at the clock. It was one o'clock in the morning, so why was someone calling his phone at this time of night. He figured it was Amber, so he decided to ignore it because her ass wasn't talking about shit. Big Lee adjusted herself on Whisper's chest, and he looked down at her and smirked. His phone began to ring again, and he glanced over at the screen. He saw that it was Byrd, so he quickly snatched it up off the nightstand.

"What's up?" Whisper answered urgently.

"Where you at?" Byrd coughed. "I just got robbed by two niggas, and I think ManMan set me up!" Whisper sat up in bed causing Big

Lee to fall on the mattress. She jumped up and was about to go off when she heard Whisper say,

"I'm gone dead that nigga!"

CHAPTER TWENTY-THREE

$\mathcal{W}$hisper instructed Byrd to come to his house. He told him to park his car in the parking spot directly behind the house, and to come inside through the back door. Byrd followed his instructions to the letter, and when he walked into Whisper's house, he and Big Lee were waiting for him with pistols in hand.

"What the fuck happened, baby?" Big Lee asked walking toward him. "They roughed your ass up good, and I think you're going to need stitches." She grabbed his chin and turned his head to the side.

"What I need to do is slap a band-aide on this shit so me and Whisper can ride!" Byrd hissed. "Them niggas knew I was coming, and they waited for me like some cowards in the apartment next door!"

"Who were you going to meet?" Whisper asked. "And did you tell someone where you were going?"

"I ain't tell nobody shit! I had just gotten into it with Lay, so I just left her house without telling her where I was going. Normally, I tell her when I'm making moves just in case some dumb shit like this happens."

"What you and Lay get into it about?" Big Lee asked nosily.

"That ain't none of your business, Ann," Whisper snapped "If you ain't gone be helpful, then go back upstairs!" Both Big Lee and Byrd looked at Whisper in shock. He glared back at her as if to say, 'say something' and her body language changed. She had rose up her chest as if she was going to say something back in defense to his statement, but when he gave her that look, Big Lee's shoulders slouched, and she sank down a few inches. "Ann, can you go upstairs in my bathroom and get the first aid kit. Also, you're probably going to have to sew up his head."

"No offense, Big Lee, but she ain't about to sew shit up right here!" Byrd declared. Both Whisper and Big Lee laughed because the expression on his face was priceless.

"Lil' nappy headed boy, sit yo' ass down on that stool and calm the fuck down!" Big Lee instructed. "You can't go to the hospital, because you don't want any paperwork attached to your name."

"What do you mean?" Byrd uttered confused. "Paperwork?" Big Lee looked over at Whisper and smiled.

"Let me school you for a second, young blood, because if you're going to marry our daughter, you're going to have to know the first thing about being a part of the Wilson Family," Big Lee explained. "It's obvious that you want some type of restitution to the situation, that's why Whisper was the first person you called; am I correct with this assumption?"

"Yes, ma'am," Byrd replied.

"And if this is the case, well you know that we're about to go fuck some shit up!"

"We?" Byrd questioned, looking confused.

"Yes, we, muthafucka!" Big Lee replied sarcastically. "You're my child now, and I don't play about mine! My reputation didn't come from wise tales like some of these other niggas around here! I put in work when needed, and I have a trail of dead bodies with this man right here, and I don't intend on letting up! That nigga ManMan has violated one too many times, and it's time that his little punk ass gets dealt with!"

"Baby, go ahead and get the kit so you can clean him up. I'm about to call Ax to see where he's at and have him come over," Whisper suggested.

"Okay, baby," Big Lee replied nonchalantly. Byrd stared at them strangely, because Big Lee was actually doing what Whisper had instructed. "Hey, Whisper."

"What's up?" Whisper replied.

"Tell Ax I said to hotbox," she uttered before disappearing out of the kitchen. Whisper knew exactly what she was talking about and a big smile came across his face.

"We about to take your ass to school, young blood! I guess we can call this your initiation into our family," Whisper gloated.

"I'm ready, Whisper, bruh, because some niggas about to feel the pain after this one!" Byrd grunted angrily. "Muthafuckas said that a nigga was salty after he found out that I was fucking with Lay, but never in a million years did I think that he would do something so scandalous like this! He straight done some bitch shit, but I got something for that ass!"

"No doubt, Byrd Man," Whisper replied with a smile. "You finna see first hand why Lay's ass is bat shit crazy!"

****

Ax had come to pick Big Lee, Whisper, and Byrd up from the house. He went around to the junkyard and picked up one of the random raggedy looking cars that they kept there for moments like this. They were still in pursuit of Geechie, and an unmarked car was the best way to ride down on a nigga if you're planning to kill them. They all ran like a champ because Ax made sure that the motor and everything was up to par. However, they would keep the dents and rust on the cars in order to make people think that they were dope fiend's rentals.

"What we gone do in this raggedy ass car?" Byrd scoffed. "The police gone catch up before we even make it off the block!"

"Get yo' dumb ass in the car, boy!" Ax scoffed. "You got me fucked up if you think this muthafucka don't go!" Everybody laughed as they approached the car. Whisper opened the front door for Big Lee, and she kissed him softly on the lips before she climbed inside. He shut the door behind her and got into the backseat directly in the rear of her. Byrd opened up the driver's side passenger door to get inside but was stopped by a bag of semi-automatic weapons and a lot of ammo. Ax looked over the back of the seat and smirked at Byrd. "Just move that shit over. Have you ever shot one of those before, youngsta?"

"Don't play, Ax! You knows how I gets down!" Byrd scoffed.

"Tru' dat!" Ax chuckled. "Just like I thought!" Byrd moved the bag over and got into the car. Whisper had given him a black ski mask and a pair of brownie gloves to cover his hands. It fucked Byrd up when he saw Big Lee come downstairs dressed in all black, and she had her ski mask rolled up like a skullcap. Her hands were covered in a pair of brownie gloves, and Whisper commented on how sexy she looked in all black. Byrd thought their asses were crazy the way they were flirting with one another. They were about to go on a straight gangsta mission, but they found time to joke and play with one another. He wondered would him and Lay be like that if they ever had to put in some work together. However, he hoped it never came down to that.

Ax drove by the gambling house to see if ManMan was there. He made a few phone calls, and no one had seen him for the past few hours. Byrd had them go by his dope house, and he ran up in there so see if ManMan had been there in last few hours. Ash, Mara's girlfriend, told him that ManMan had stopped by there when he had left the hospital. She said that he was pissed off and looking for Byrd, because of the shit that had happened with Lay and Ew Baby. Ash said ManMan was going on and on about how Byrd just stood there and let 'them bitches' fuck him up with a bat. She said ManMan had his arm in a sling and complained of having three broken ribs. She mentioned that one of his eyes was black, and he had a bunch of bruises all over his face. Byrd didn't give a fuck about that and just wanted to know if she'd seen him. Byrd told Ash to get the locks changed before the morning was up, and he would be by later to get a key. He told her that ManMan or any of his cronies weren't allowed at the house, and if anyone of them showed up, to call him.

Ax decided to drive over to ManMan's house that was further on the west side of the city. Byrd was surprised that Ax knew about this house, because ManMan rarely mentioned it. However, Ax spent a lot of money at the gambling house, and sometimes ManMan hosted exclusive games at his spot.

"He ain't here," Byrd said frankly. "The television ain't on in the room upstairs, so that nigga ain't here."

"What the fuck does that mean?" Whisper asked sarcastically. "How much money did they get you for?" Byrd looked at him with a stupid expression on his face.

"They got me for a brick and a few thousand dollars that I had in my pocket," he replied.

"Why are you walking around with all of that shit?" Big Lee scoffed. "You better be happy that the cops didn't pull your dumb ass over!"

"I was on my way to sell a nigga the brick," Byrd replied arrogantly. "I ain't no nickel and dime ass lil' nigga! I make money moves all across this city!"

"And yo' stupid ass got hit tu-niggghhhttt!" Big Lee shot back. Ax and Whisper laughed while Byrd stewed in the backseat. "Don't get mad, baby, because it happens to the best of them. I've had niggas steal from me before, so no one is safe."

"And you have a jar of their fingers hidden in the refrigerator from them niggas too," Whisper added.

"What?" Byrd shouted. Big Lee turned around and smiled at him.

"That's right! If I catch yo' ass stealing from me, I have Teke cut them muthafuckas off, and I put them in a jar," Big Lee explained. Byrd scrunched his face up with the mere thought of the pain. He'd heard myths about this so called jar, but to have his one day mother-in-law admit that she had one ended up being potentially the highlight of his night.

"So what are we going to do?" Byrd asked frustrated. "It's four o'clock in the morning, and we ain't done shit!" Big Lee looked behind her and frowned at Byrd.

"Now I let your lil' ass slide with the cursing when you first came to Whisper's house, because I empathize with your situation. However, I ain't gone keep sitting here listening to you utter off four letter words, so you better check self and respect my swagger!"

"My fault, Big Lee, but I'm just completely pissed the fu---"

"We know that you're pissed, Byrd Man," Ax interrupted. "That's why we're going to make this shit count!" Ax parked in front of ManMan's house and popped the trunk. "Ski mask," he said before he got out of the car. All of them pulled them down and got out the car while Ax went around to the trunk. Big Lee and Whisper pulled out their pistols, and Byrd pulled his out because he was following their lead. Ax proceeded to the front door with a gas can in his hand. Byrd wasn't sure what Ax was about to do, but whatever the fuck it was he was definitely with it.

Whisper kicked in the front door, and they rushed inside like a synchronized swat team. They all spread throughout the house and searched the place, but there wasn't anyone there presently. Byrd had found the bloody clothes that ManMan had on earlier sitting in the middle of the floor. It was evident that he'd been there, and Byrd wondered was this where ManMan had placed the call to him. Byrd walked over to the closet and opened up the door. He noticed that it looked like someone was in a hurry. There were clothes and shoeboxes thrown all over the floor, and the lock box where ManMan kept all of his important papers were gone. This solidified the fact that ManMan had set Byrd up, and that's why he got the fuck out of dodge like he did.

"C'mon, Byrd," said Whisper standing in the doorway. "It's time for us to go!"

"That muthafucka's been here, and it seems like he's gone on a vacation," Byrd informed him. "But I'm gone catch that son of a bitch!"

"Most definitely!" Whisper assured him. "'Cause that nigga's gonna wanna collect his money, and that's when we're going to get that ass together!"

Whisper and Byrd walked back downstairs where Big Lee and Ax were waiting by the door. The air reeked of gasoline, and Byrd put his arm up against his nose and mouth, because the fumes were quite strong. Ax had a lighter in his hand and flipped up the top off of it. Next, he looked at everyone with a devilish smile on his face because he was ready to have some fun.

"Let's get the fuck out of here, because I'm about to blow this bitch up!" Ax yelled out in excitement.

"We ain't done no arson in a long time," Big Lee announced proudly. "It's been maybe about four years?"

"Actually, it's been about five," Whisper corrected her. "Remember Cam almost caught his pants leg on fire because some of the gasoline spilled on it while he was pouring it around the house." There was a few seconds of quiet because they all felt some type of way as they thought about their little brother. "C'mon, Ann," Whisper uttered. "Byrd, you bring your ass on too!" They all walked out to the car while Ax remained inside. He flicked the lighter and a flame jumped up. He threw it on the floor then walked out before the entire house was engulfed in flames.

CHAPTER TWENTY-FOUR

*L*ay woke up and checked her phone for a message from Byrd. She saw that she had missed his call, and felt a bit relieved, but saddened that she had fell asleep. He left in haste last night, and they didn't get an opportunity to resolve their conflict. However, Lay made sure that she called Reed and had an uncomfortable conversation with him that resulted in being hung up on.

Lay washed her face, brushed her teeth, and wiped off her vital parts before putting on clothes and heading to her mother's house. Ew Baby's door was closed, so she assumed that she and Ax were still in there sleeping. It was crazy how she found out that they were a couple last night, but so much random craziness had been happening that nothing would surprise her at this point. She walked down the steps and stopped at the window. She hit her remote start to warm up her car. Nothing says good morning like a delicious breakfast, and she knew that Whisper or her mama always had something whipped up, so she was about to make her way over there to get her a plate of food.

Lay walked into her mother's house, and it was quiet as a mouse. She walked into the kitchen, and there was no trace of her mother or

Whisper. She decided to go upstairs to see if they were still in bed, but when she got to her mother's room, the door was wide open. A sudden panic came across Lay, because it was unusual for her mother not to be there, and if Big Lee had decided to go to the big house, she would have called or messaged Lay to let her know that she'd gone. Lay pulled out her phone, dialed her mother's number, and waited impatiently until she answered.

"Hey, baby girl. Good Morning."

"Mama, where you at?" Lay asked anxiously. "I'm at your house, but you're not here!"

"Calm down, baby girl. I'm at your daddy's house," Big Lee replied.

"My daddy's in…" Lay paused for a moment and put her hand against her forehead. "You're up the street?"

"Ain't that where yo' daddy lives?" Big Lee asked sarcastically.

"Yeah," Lay replied. "But I have to get used to the whole concept of Whisper being my real father. Did he cook?" Big Lee laughed as she looked across the table at Byrd.

"Yes, he cooked," she replied. "Why don't you come join us? We have a guest I think you might like to see."

"I doubt that," Lay scoffed. "But here I come."

Lay left her mother's house and headed to her daddy's. It was only three doors down, so she didn't have that far to travel. She thought it was cute that they were over Whisper's house because they always spent time at Big Lee's. She opened the gate and walked into the yard, then proceeded up the steps to the front door. Whisper was standing in the doorway watching Lay walk down the street. He had his pistol in his hand, and Lay thought that his behavior was unusual.

"Good morning, princess," said Whisper holding the door open.

"Good morning, Daddy," she replied with a big smile. Whisper matched her smile as she walked through the door, and Lay stopped to hug him because this had become a ritual for them whenever they see each other for the first time. Whisper kissed the top of Lay's head and closed the door behind them. "What did you cook for breakfast this morning?"

"Is that why you brought your hungry ass down the street?" Whisper joked.

"You know I come over for breakfast all the time, so don't do me, Whisper!" Lay shot back. "Plus, I need to talk to my mama about something anyway." They were headed toward the kitchen and Lay stopped short of the door when she saw Byrd sitting at the table with Big Lee eating breakfast. "What are you doing here?" Lay asked with a confused look on her face.

"Good morning to you, too," Big Lee shot back, frowning. "I taught you manners in hopes that you would use them!"

"I'm sorry," Lay apologized, walking into the room. "Good morning, Mama. Good morning, Byrd. What are you doing here?" A smirk spread across Byrd's face as he watched Lay take off her coat.

"I'm having breakfast with my soon to be in-laws," Byrd replied. He got up from his seat and pulled the chair out next to him. Lay walked up to him and placed her coat on the back of the chair. He grabbed her by the waist and pulled her into him.

"Wait a minute," Lay said putting her hands against his chest. "What happened to your face… and why is there blood all over your t-shirt?" Byrd looked over at Big Lee and Whisper then back at Lay.

"I got robbed last night when I went to make that sale," Byrd explained. "There were two niggas waiting for me, and they jumped me when I walked up to the house."

"Who were you going to meet, and where were you meeting them at?" Lay questioned angrily.

"Baby, sit down," Byrd suggested. He kissed Lay's lips quickly and ushered her into the chair. He sat down next to her, grabbed her hand, and squeezed it because he knew she was about to go off. "I was going to meet ManMan to sell a brick to some dude he had waiting. I went over to the gambling house, and two niggas robbed me."

"So that bitch ass nigga had you set up?" Lay spat. She looked over at Big Lee. "Sorry, Mama!" Big Lee and Whisper looked at Lay and chuckled.

"So yo' mama is all that you see sitting here?" Whisper asked, setting a plate of bacon, eggs, pancakes, and grits in front of her.

"I'm sorry, Whisper," Lay apologized. "I have to get used to you being my father, so don't take it personal."

"I won't," he replied. "However, don't you go grilling this boy about what happened to him last night! We took care of it, even though it's not over." Lay looked at her father with a confused look on her face.

"What is that supposed to mean?" Lay uttered. "And how did you end up over here, Byrd?" Byrd put his fork down and chewed up the food he had in his mouth.

"Last night after I got robbed, I didn't know who to call, so I hit Whisper up," Byrd explained. "I told him what happened, and he said to come over here."

"Why didn't you call me?" Lay asked. "I knew something bad had happened because my stomach felt weird all night."

"Are you sure it's not from our argument earlier?" he questioned. "And I did call you last night. Did you see a missed call from me on your phone this morning?" Lay looked at him stupidly.

"Yeah, I saw it," she replied in a snippy tone. "And I was over our argument the moment you left my house. I can't believe ManMan's stupid butt set you up!"

"I can't believe it either, but he'll have a big surprise waiting on him when he goes to his house," Byrd gloated.

"What do you mean?" Lay asked confused. Byrd looked over at Big Lee and Whisper with a proud expression on his face.

"After I came over here to talk to Whisper, your mother cleaned up my face and put a few stitches over my eye," Byrd explained.

"That's why there's a band-aide there?" Lay asked, touching the spot.

"Yes, but let me finish telling you what happened," Byrd added. He looked over at Lay's parents then back at her. "Your mother was pissed about what happened, and I was ready to ride down on the nigga with my eye bleeding and everything. Whisper calmed me down and convinced me to get my face stitched up, and while your mama patched me up, your daddy made a call to Ax."

"But no one thought to call me?" Lay interjected angrily. "All of this shit was going on, and no one thought to call me?" She glared over at her parents vehemently, because she felt a bit betrayed by them. "I don't believe the both of you! Byrd is my man, and no one thought to call to tell me what was going on!"

"Shit was happening so fast, Lay, that it never crossed my mind," Whisper replied. "The only thing I was focused on was going to get that nigga, ManMan."

"What the fuck was you gone do?" Big Lee scoffed. "Byrd called your father because he felt that Whisper was the best person to help him handle the situation."

"That doesn't matter! Byrd is my boyfriend, and I feel like someone should have called me! I would have gone to help Byrd find ManMan!" Lay ranted. "We're supposed to be in this thing together, Byrd. I can't believe you didn't call me, or at least send me a text message. Especially the way you seem to really be into reading them! The hell with that! You should have come to my house!"

"What is that supposed to mean?" Byrd scoffed. "You're the one that's got some nigga texting you, talking about how much he misses and loves you!" Whisper and Big Lee looked at the both of them uncomfortably. They didn't want to be in the middle of their daughter's relationship, but Big Lee wanted to know what was going on. She remembered that Byrd had mentioned that they had gotten into it, but Whisper stopped Big Lee from getting into their business, so she didn't know what had happened.

"Let's just eat our food," Big Lee suggested. "Byrd is safe, and we handled the situation. That should be good enough for now. Lay, Mama's sorry for not calling you, and I will be more conscious of your feelings in the future." Lay cut her eyes at her mother because she was pissed.

"Will you?" Lay shot back. "You're good at lying and keeping secrets from me, so I don't know why I would think that you would be considerate of my feelings!" Big Lee looked at her daughter in disbelief. "I mean, you lied to both Whisper and I about him being my father for years, so why would this be any different. I bet you weren't even going to tell me what happened, and I would have had to find out everything from Byrd!"

"That's not fair, Lay," Byrd scoffed. "You can't get mad at your mother, because I didn't call and tell you!"

"Yes I can!" Lay spat back. "She should have had enough respect for our relationship to call and tell me that you were with her and had been hurt!"

"Don't you think your ass is being a bit over dramatic," Big Lee spat. "There were reasons why I kept the truth about Whisper being your father from you, and this situation is nothing like that! You're comparing apples and oranges, so get a grip, little girl!"

"See that's part of the problem right there! I'm not a little girl, and I wish you would stop treating me like one!" Lay demanded. "You always keep shit from me, and I'm left stuck looking stupid when it comes to pass!"

"You better watch your mouth, Lay, because I'm not beyond smacking the shit out of you in front of your boooy friend!" Big Lee spat. "Now I can understand that your upset with me, but I be damned if you're going to sit here and disrespect me!"

"I---"

"You heard what the fuck I said!" Big Lee interrupted and jumped up from the table. She slammed her fist down hard against it and stared at Lay with fire in her eyes. Lay stared at her mother for a second and tears welled up in her eyes. Lay looked over at Byrd, who had a surprised look on his face, then she turned to face Whisper. He looked at her sorrowfully because he knew where this argument was headed.

"You always got to exert your power, don't you," Lay stammered. "And you don't care who you embarrass in the process! Well I'm not Whisper, and I don't have to put up with this shit! Since you're so eager to help my man, then he can take my place in this family!" Lay grabbed her coat off the back of her chair and stormed out of the kitchen. Tears were streaming down her face, and everyone sat frozen for a second because things went wrong so fast. Big Lee looked at Whisper with a frustrated expression on her face, and Byrd got up from his seat to go after Lay.

"Make sure she's okay," Big Lee said solemnly. "That little girl gets on my got damn last nerve! She feels like she's the one in charge, but I beg to differ!"

"I think you were the one being over dramatic this time, Ann," Whisper replied. "You just embarrassed her in front of her guy, and you know how you feel when people do that to you!"

"She ain't about to sit up here and disrespect me, Whisper!"

"I get that part but take a look at her position. You would have been super pissed if the shoe was on the other foot and no one called you if something happened to me! She gets her flare for dramatics from you, but this time you get the Emmy for your performance," Whisper offered. He got up from the table and started to collect the plates. He wasn't sure how long this thing between Big Lee and Lay was going to last, but he was going to stay out of it and let them figure this shit out.

CHAPTER TWENTY-FIVE

$\mathcal{E}$w Baby rolled over and stared at Ax while he slept. She couldn't believe some of the stuff he had told her, but it gave her a better understanding of why he was insane. Ax had done a lot of shit to people in his short life. He had older brothers already deep into the gang life when he became a teenager that he was in by association. Ew Baby had been on missions with Ax, and she'd even witness him killing a few people, but she loved him deep and would never snitch on him. She wondered where he had disappeared too last night because he jumped out of bed and left abruptly. However, when he called and told her to open the door, butterflies rose up in her stomach with excitement. She wondered why he reeked of gasoline when he came into the house, but she didn't bother to ask because he would tell her soon enough.

Ew Baby was a bit thrown off last night when Ax didn't want to have sex. He'd damn near had his dick inside her last week, but now all of a sudden shit had changed. She stared at his features, wondering if she had a baby by him, whom would it look like. She loved his nose and soft full lips. They were the same complexion, so they would have a beautiful brown baby. She wanted to feel Ax inside of her and waiting just might be more of challenge than she thought.

Ew Baby reached down and cupped Ax's manhood in her hand. She held it for a second to see if he would react. When he didn't flinch, Ew Baby knew that he was deep into his sleep. A sinister smile came across her face as an idea popped into her brain. She slid down the mattress and stopped when she came face to face with Ax's dick. He didn't have a long pecker, but the thick girth made up for it. He would definitely stretch a pussy out and Ew Baby could barely stand it. She stroked it slowly as her mouth salivated at the thought of putting it in her mouth. She waited with baited breath because she wanted him to respond invitingly. Patience wasn't one of Ew Baby's strongest points, and she could no longer wait for him to come around.

Ew Baby grabbed the elastic waistband of Ax's underwear, and his dick fell out in her face. A satisfying grin came across her mouth as she licked her lips hungrily. Ew Baby licked around the head of it a few times then plunged it inside of her mouth. It was so easy to deep throat him that she knew that Ax would be in love with her head instantly. She continued to go up and down, occasionally swirling her tongue around the tip. Ax cupped her head and moaned as Ew Baby sucked her jaws in; giving him a tighter sensation around his dick. He grabbed the back of her weave and pulled, and Ew Baby giggled at his reaction. She cupped his ass and squeezed with one hand while the other massaged his balls gently.

"Ah damn, Ew Baby!" Ax groaned. "I knew you sucked good dick, but you ain't never sucked my dick like this!" She didn't let his words distract her, because she was on a mission to make this nigga cum, hard! Once his toes curled and body shook from an Ew Baby dick suck, she would be satisfied with her work. "I'm about to nut!" he stammered as his sack tightened in her hand. Ew Baby tightened the grip with her jaws and went down once more and made sure the tip touched her tonsils. That was the finishing move that sent Ax howling like a wolf. He curled his toes and stretched out stiffly while Ew Baby gobbled up his cum like a beast. She licked and slurped as she sucked the head of his rod hungrily. She swallowed all of his offerings and continued to work for more. Ax couldn't take any more of this bomb ass head, so he pulled Ew Baby up off of him by her hair. She laughed as she grabbed a hold with her hand and stoked it vigorously as more of his man milk spat out. "You are a beast, Ew Baby!" Ax declared. He put his hands on the side of her face and kissed her nastily on the lips. He sucked the bottom one as she continued to pleasure him with her hand, and at one point, he had to breath heavily because another eruption was about to occur. "I'm about to nut again…" Ax said breathlessly against Ew Baby's lips.

"Good," she replied, and kissed his lips quickly. Ew Baby went back down and took him in her mouth once more, then sucked real hard until he exploded, yet again, down her throat. She loved how Ax shook in her mouth, and now she was satisfied with herself. If Patricia didn't teach her nothing else, she taught her daughter that a good dick suck and a well fed man would keep you in pocket with a nigga for sure.

"Giiiirrrrllll!" Ax shouted, enthusiastically. "I'm gone marry yo' black ass the way you suck a nigga's dick!" Ew Baby laughed as Ax wrapped his arm around her neck and kissed her in the center of her forehead. "I love you, Ew Baby, and you're finally all mine!" He pressed his lips firmly against hers and she savored the moment. His words were music to her ears, and he didn't have to worry about shit, because she wasn't going anywhere! "And I'm gone tell you another thing," he added. He stared lovingly into her eyes, but then a crazed glare came across his. He grabbed her by the throat and squeezed it a bit too tight for her liking. "If I ever catch you with another nigga, I'm gon' fuck you up! If I catch you fucking or sucking another nigga, I'm gone fuck you up! I don't want you socializing or conversing with no nigga! Do I make myself clear?" Ew Baby didn't flinch, because she had been through a lot in her young, twenty-one-year-old life. Big Daddy used to choke her like this when he would do his business in her, and eventually she would ask him to squeeze harder in hopes that he would accidently kill her. However, her center tingled with Ax's declaration of love. Her insides were going insane while her center dripped with anticipation.

"Fuck me, Ax," Ew Baby moaned. "I can't wait!" Her eyes widened, and she licked her lips lustfully. Ax could see that she was getting off by him choking her, and his dick instantly got rock hard. "Fuck me like there's no tomorrow! I gotta have you inside of me!"

"That pussy's wet, ain't it," Ax groaned lustfully.

"Yes…"

"You want this dick inside of you badly, huh?" he questioned.

"Yes…" Ew Baby whispered, leaning her head back. She grabbed his wrist, and Ax tightened his grip. Ew Baby smiled greedily, and this sent Ax over the edge.

He flipped Ew Baby on her back and ripped her nightgown off of her body. He stared at her tattoo-covered breast and smirked at the red roses that she had up under her breast. They went from one side to the other, and he thought it was the sexiest tattoo that he'd ever seen. He grabbed the tip of his erection and rubbed it against her folds. It didn't take much for him to ease right in, because as soon as his head met the opening, it instantly went inside and sank down in it.

"Oh shit, Ew Baby!" Ax called out urgently. He pushed down and came back up a few times as the soft warm feeling of her walls engulfed his stiffness. He leaned down and kissed her lips nastily. He didn't expect her pussy to feel this good. Everybody knew how promiscuous Ew Baby was at an early age, and she hadn't let up in her twenties. Ax had heard about her being run through by several men, so he already had some preconceived notions. He continued to stroke her methodically, and the moans and groans that escaped her lips let him know that she was enjoying her dick down. "Whose pussy is this, Ew Baby?" Ax asked sternly.

"It's your pussy, Axel," she mumbled, biting her bottom lip. He'd hit the bottom a couple of times forcefully, and she enjoyed the pleasure of his pain. "I am devoted to you, Ax, and no one will tear us apart!" Ax stared down at her with a pleased smile on his face. He saw the sincerity in Ew Baby's eyes and when tears filled the bottom of them, he knew that she was spent.

"I love you," Ax mumbled and kissed her lips hard. They continued to fuck passionately until both of them came hard! Ew Baby withered first and shook as her orgasm sent shivers through her body. Ax continued to lay it down until his third nut shot inside of Ew Baby's womb, and he collapsed on top of her in exhaustion.

Ew Baby had gone to the bathroom to get a hot washcloth to wipe Ax off. He wasn't ready to get in the shower, and he wanted to lay up and cuddle for a while before he had to leave for work. She walked up to the door and stopped when she heard Ax on the phone. She wondered whom he was talking too because the conversation seemed a little too cozy for her liking. Also, Ax had the nerve to have the phone on speaker.

"You know I miss you, so why you playin'?" Ax chuckled.

"I bet you're probably laid up with some pussy right now, ain't you?" Angie teased. "You ain't got me fooled, Ax, and I bet I know who you're with." Ax laughed as he grabbed two blue capsules out of his pocket. He broke one open and sniffed it quickly then did the same thing in the other one. Ew Baby watched in horror as the love of her life sat on the edge of her bed and snorted dope up his nose. The fact that he was talking to some other bitch on the phone didn't matter, because this nigga really violated by what he'd just done!

"What the fuck you doin'?" Ew Baby shouted as she barged into the room. Ax looked at her and smiled, wiping his nose. "And who the fuck are you talking too?"

"Sounds like you're about to have some problems. I'm going to let you go," Angie uttered then laughed. "You're about to get your ass beat!"

"It ain't nothing like that, sweetie," Ax replied, smiling at Ew Baby.

"Who the fuck are you talking to, Ax?" Ew Baby shouted. She picked up a cup of water off her desk and threw it on Ax. "Answer me got damn it!"

"Amanda, I'll holla." Ax hung up the phone and stared at Ew Baby amused. "Why are you all hostile and shit?"

"Because your ass is straight aggy, and I'm going to end up killing you, Axel!" Ew Baby shouted. "I saw you snort that shit up your nose, and I be damned if I fuck with a hop head!"

"Ew Baby, calm your ass down!" Ax replied firmly. "I ain't no fucking hop head, and I can explain what you just saw."

"I just bet you can!" she shouted disgruntled. "My mama's a fucking dope fiend, and I be damned if I fuck with one! How could you trick me into your arms then drop a bomb like this on me!" Ew Baby was hysterical and tears fell down her face uncontrollably. She wanted to hurt Ax for doing this to her, but she stood paralyzed in place. Ax got up off the bed and grabbed his pants off the floor. He reached into his pocket and pulled out a prescription bottle then walked up to Ew Baby.

"Calm yo' stupid ass down!" Ax barked. He put the bottle in front of Ew Baby's face so she could read it. "What you saw me sniffing was my medicine. I've been suffering from migraine headaches ever since Cam was killed, and the doctor prescribed me this medicine, because I can't swallow pills." The prescription had his full name on it along with a refill number at the bottom. The label read Onzetra Xsail.

"What the fuck is this?" Ew Baby spat, snatching the bottle out of his hand. She opened it up and looked inside. "I don't understand."

"I just told you the fucking truth! I go to a doctor named Dr. Alfonso Warren, and he was the one who gave me these," Ax explained.

"I know it looks suspect, but I promise you, I ain't on no dope." Ew Baby looked at him skeptically.

"So if you're not on dope, that's cool," Ew Baby uttered. "But who the fuck was that bitch you were talking to on the phone!" Ax held his head down and laughed.

"There's no winning with you!"

"Fuck naw," Ew Baby snapped. Ax looked at her as if he could see right through her, and he found her jealousy a bit cute.

"She's just some bitch that I'm fucking with on a business tip," Ax replied nonchalantly. "She fucks with that nigga, Cecil, and I want to get the drop on his ass when he gets out of prison." Ew Baby looked at her strangely.

"Lay told me that nigga's my daddy, but I don't know if I should believe it," Ew Baby mentioned.

"The nigga Cecil is yo' daddy, but I think you need to talk to my sister about that shit," Ax replied. "Ew Baby, I promise that I won't do anything to hurt you." He cupped the back of her head and stared into her eyes. "Let's go lie back down, and I will explain everything to you." He rested his forehead against hers. "Can we just do that?" Ew Baby grabbed his wrist and squeezed.

"Yes," she whispered breathlessly then they kissed.

CHAPTER TWENTY-SIX

*B*yrd ran out of the house after Lay, and she was already halfway up the block. She was running so fast that it was hard for Byrd to catch her, but he put up a chase trying catch her. Lay turned the corner of Aldine and was almost at home when Byrd finally caught up with her. He was breathing heavily with just a t-shirt and jeans on, and the cold spring air had him shaking.

"Lay, wait a minute!" Byrd insisted, grabbing her by the shoulder. "You're totally overreacting like usual, and I'm not going to let you do this!"

"Do what?" she snapped, turning around to face him. "I'm tired of my mama lying to me! She has all these secrets that's going to tear our family apart!"

"How do figure that?" Byrd questioned hastily. "Everything that your mother did was to protect you. Plus, it doesn't matter what happened in the past. What you need to concentrate on is the present. She didn't have to tell your ass shit, and you would have went on not knowing shit!"

"Why did you run to them?" Lay stammered. "You should have come to me! You should have come to me!"

"For what, Lay? So we could ride down on ManMan and handle the shit!"

"You got damn right!" she shouted back. "I'm supposed to be the one to have your back! I'm your ride or die! I would dead that nigga if it meant that you would be safe! I have no allegiance to that nigga! I've fucked niggas up before!"

"But have you killed a man before, Lay? Do you know what it feels like to take a person's life in a split second and see them take their last breath?" Lay stared at him angrily, but she could see that he was freezing. There were goose bumps all over his arms, and his voice shivered when he talked.

"Why did you leave out without a jacket?" Lay fussed. "Your ass is going to be sick from trying to be a superhero!"

"Fuck you, Lay!" Byrd shot back. "Now come the fuck on so we can go in the house!" He wrapped his arm around Lay's neck and put her in a headlock. She wrapped her arm around his waist and giggled as they walked up the street. She was mad at her mother for not calling her about Byrd, but the real reason why she was mad now had everything to do with her embarrassing Lay in front of her man.

Lay and Byrd walked into the house, and Ew Baby had just walked downstairs. She was about to cook breakfast while Ax took a shower because he had to get to the garage to work. He had been on a long hiatus, and it was time for him to get some normalcy back into his life. She looked at them crazily because Byrd wasn't wearing a jacket.

"Nigga, what's wrong with you?" Ew Baby questioned. "Why you don't have on a jacket? It's cold as fuck outside!"

"You tellin' me!" Byrd replied, shivering. "I would have had it if this knuckle head wouldn't have ran out of Whisper's house."

"Why did you run out of Whisper's house?" Ew Baby asked nosily. Lay looked over at Byrd and cut her eyes at him.

"Because yo' mama was on another one of her trips and straight embarrassed me in front of Byrd!" Lay explained.

"What?" Ew Baby scoffed. "You know she do the most!"

"The most," Byrd echoed.

"The fucking most!" Lay insisted. "But it's yo' fault, Byrd, 'cause you should have called me before you dialed any other number!"

"I heard you got robbed last night, and it was ManMan's punk ass that set it up!" Ew Baby mentioned frankly.

"How the fuck do you know?" Lay hissed.

"Because Ax told me this morning, after we---"

"Never mind!" Lay interrupted. "Did that really happen last night?"

"Yes it did," Ew Baby replied happily. "But it actually didn't happen until this morning. You didn't hear Ax when he left last night?"

"No," Lay replied confused. "I was passed the fuck out because my ass was tired."

"Naw, bae. It was 'cause I knocked the bottom out of that pussy last night!" Byrd gloated. He grabbed Lay, squeezed her ass with both hands, then kissed her tenderly on the nape of her neck.

"Boy, you silly!" Lay giggled as he continued to nibble on her neck. "But for real, Byrd… You violated by leaving me out of the loop.

I'm your future wife; your ride or die forever, baby! You were being inconsiderate, and I didn't appreciate that shit at all!"

"If you gone be mad then be mad, Lay, I don't give a fuck! I refuse to put your life at risk just to stroke your ego," Byrd fussed.

"Stroke my ego? Well ain't that a bitch!" Lay hissed. "Why does my ego have anything to do with this, Byrd? Why can't it be about the principle of the matter? I wanted you to call me first because, what if you were shot or something," she stammered. "Worse than that… what if you were dying?" A single tear ran down her face, and she quickly wiped it away.

"I understand where you're coming from now, but I stand on the decision that I made," Byrd affirmed. "I called the best man for the job, and Whisper was ready and with it!"

"Wasn't he?" Ax added, walking into the kitchen. "He and my sister looked all cute and shit with their son-in-law in tow to go handle his beef. They had on matching ski mask and brownie gloves. Shit, I think they all had matching Glocks, too!" Everyone laughed as Ax made jokes, but Byrd didn't find that shit too funny. He felt like Ax was sending jabs at him as if he couldn't handle the shit on his own.

"Don't get it twisted, I could have handle my own smoke, but I knew it was several muthafuckas involved," Byrd insisted.

"Byrd Man, I know you are the truth," Ax assured him. "So don't get so defensive when I yank yo' chain." Ax winked at him and made his way over to Ew Baby. "I got to go, baby. I'll call you in a bit."

"Ok Ax, but don't forget I have to work tonight," Ew Baby reminded him. "I haven't worked in over a week, and my pockets are in need of some funds." Ax frowned at Ew Baby and reached into his pocket.

"You ain't never broke," he hissed and peeled a few big faces off the wad of cash in his hand. "If you need something then ask, Ew Baby. I told you this is us!" He kissed her lips tenderly and held it for a few seconds. Lay stared at them strangely, because she couldn't believe that they were a couple.

"Damn, Ew Baby! Don't hurt 'em like that!" Byrd teased. "Niggas gone have to respect you now that Axel Wilson is your man!"

"You got that right!" Ax second. "And I'm gone dead any muthafucka that steps out of line with her!" Ew Baby smiled proudly as she stood next to Ax. Lay walked by and pushed her on the shoulder to move her out of the way.

"Fuck Ew Baby!" Lay interjected. "Don't nobody care about y'all!"

"Sounds like a bitch is jea-lous!" Ew Baby shot back.

"My baby ain't got shit to be jealous about! We got that Jay and Bee type of love!" Byrd scoffed. Lay damn near fell trying to turn around to look at him.

"No you didn't, nigga, after you forgot to call me last night!" Lay protested.

"I called you, but yo' punk ass ain't answer! Did you even listen to the message that I left for you?" Lay was about to say something smart, but she stopped in her tracks.

"No, I didn't listen to my message," she admitted.

"Okay then, so shut the fuck up talking about it! I didn't call you, so get the fuck over it! I'll consider remembering it next time two niggas decide to jump out and rob me!" Byrd snapped angrily. Everyone stared at him dumbfounded because it was obvious that he was tired of hearing the shit. Lay saw the look on his face, and she took a cue from earlier. She was tired of arguing with Byrd and figured that was the reason he might have gotten robbed. He was off of his game, because they had just got finished arguing before he left. This relationship shit was a lot of work, and Lay had a lot to learn about being the 'woman' in their relationship.

"Are you hungry, Byrd?" Lay asked nonchalantly. "I have some leftover Chinese food in the fridge, and I was going to scramble up some more eggs to put with it."

"Yeah, I'm hungry, but I need to go back around the corner to get my car," Byrd explained. "I have to go down to my place to check on some shit."

"You want me to go with you?" Lay offered. He studied her face for a second and got a kick out of this humbled Lay.

"Yeah, I want you to ride with me," Byrd replied. "We can stop off somewhere and pick up some food before we go in." A smile came across Lay's face, and she looked at Byrd lustfully.

"I know what that look means," Ax teased. "Let me go to work." He kissed Ew Baby quickly then walked out of the kitchen.

"Somebody's nose is wide open!" Lay sang joyfully.

"Yes it is, and your girl is in love!" Ew Baby sang. "Sweet love…"

CHAPTER TWENTY-SEVEN

*M*anMan nervously walked into the gambling house through the back door. He called Big Daddy and told him to meet him there but mentioned not to let anyone know where he was going. The alarm company notified ManMan that his house had caught on fire. They mentioned that they thought it might have been arson, and ManMan knew exactly who might have done it. He knew there were going to be repercussions behind his actions, but he figured he would be able to lie his way out of it since Byrd was his best friend. Needless to say, that wasn't the case.

Big Daddy was sitting on the couch watching television when ManMan came strolling into the room. He walked over to the front window and peeked out of the blinds. Big Daddy watched as ManMan continued to stare out into the distance, and he noticed the gun on ManMan's waist. Big Daddy heard that Ew Baby and Lay beat the shit out of ManMan, and this was the first time that he'd seen him.

"What's so urgent that you had me rush around here, only to wait on you for an hour?" Big Daddy complained. "I was about to eat when you called me---"

"As big as your ass is, you can stand to miss a meal!" ManMan spat annoyed. "We're going to have to shut the gambling house down for a while. Don't ask me how long, because I don't know."

"Does this have anything to do with Byrd getting robbed last night?" Big Daddy questioned.

"How do you know about that?" ManMan uttered. He turned to face Big Daddy with a strange look on his face.

"It's all around the neighborhood and everyone's buzzing about it," Big Daddy replied. "Old man Carl came by the house this morning to get his morning bump, and he told me about it. I heard they got Byrd for a whole thang and apparently he was coming to meet you. Did you have something to do with it?"

"What the fuck you think?" ManMan snapped.

"I don't know what to think," Big Daddy replied. "He was coming over here to see you, so whether you did it or not, you're guilty by association." ManMan looked at Big Daddy with a disgusted look on his face because he knew the statement was true. Why did he suggest that Byrd come to the gambling house? That was a classic rookie mistake.

"I ain't have shit to do with it, and I waited for his ass for a long time! If he got robbed outside of here, why didn't he knock on the damn door?" ManMan offered. "I'll tell you why, because he's lying about the whole thing!"

"If he's lying, then why are you hiding and shutting down the gambling house?" Big Daddy asked confused. "You're making yourself look guilty by doing it!"

"Have you seen Booker hanging around the neighborhood?" ManMan asked in an annoyed tone. "He owes me some money and I need to find his ass asap!"

"You didn't hear?" Big Daddy uttered, sounding surprised. "They found Booker dead up at the park this morning!"

"Byrd had gotten to him?" ManMan called out.

"Naw! That nigga overdosed," Big Daddy replied. "He still had the needle in his arm." ManMan looked at him wearily because that's whom he put on the lick. ManMan knew it was a fatal mistake when Booker said that he was going to get Geechie to help him, and it was obvious that his suspicion was correct.

"That's fucked up! I had loaned that muthafucka fifty dollars, and there's no way I'm going to get that shit now!" ManMan hissed.

"You're a petty muthafucka." Big Daddy chuckled at ManMan, but he tripped off of how jittery ManMan was acting. "Why don't you go to your house and hide out. Muthafuckas don't know about that spot." ManMan cut his eyes at Big Daddy.

"It got burned down last night, and I know that nigga Byrd had something to do with it," ManMan hissed. "I can't believe a muthafucka put me into this shit!"

"That's fucked up! If you didn't have anything to do with it, then all you have to do is tell Byrd who it was you were getting the dope for," Big Daddy suggested. "You've been up under a lot stress. How is your arm and ribs feeling?"

"Nigga, they hurt! Your stepdaughter and her friend have fucked up a lot of shit in my life! That bitch Lay has fucked Byrd's head up, and

I don't believe that things will ever be the same between me and my best friend again!"

"Patricia said you jumped on Ew Baby, and that's why they beat yo' ass," Big Daddy offered. "I think you should be happy that the girls handled you because if it were Big Lee, she probably would have cut your hands off!"

"Maaaaannn, fuck all of them!" ManMan hissed angrily. "I'm not scared of them!"

"So why are you hiding?" Big Daddy asked curiously. "'Cause it looks like you're ass is scared to me!" ManMan glared at Big Daddy angrily.

"I'm not scared of shit! I'm just trying to figure out what I'm going to do next because there's a lot of fucked up shit that has occurred, and I need to stay way ahead of the game!"

Later That Night

Big Lee walked into the Gateway with Teke in tow. They had been out riding around the neighborhood, because a friend of Teke's had told him that Geechie was hanging out at a house around the corner from the lounge. Big Lee was pissed because she had given out plenty of dope to the fiends for information, and no one bothered to come tell her this tidbit of information. It wasn't surprising to her that Byrd had gotten robbed last night because that's Geechie's ammo. She couldn't figure out how ManMan and Geechie had hooked up, but she knew that the both of them were in bed together.

Lay saw her mother headed toward the bar, so she went into

the cooler, and got her mother a bottle of water. She set it down on the counter where Big Lee always sat, and she poured her shot of tequila with a lime on the edge of the glass. Lay was still pissed at her mother, and she didn't want to talk to her right now. She wanted her mother to treat her like an adult and stop embarrassing her as if she were anything less.

"KeKe, I'm about to go wait tables," Lay told her picking up a tray.

"You just want to go around there with that lil' boy," KeKe teased.

"That's a man, baa-by," Lay scoffed. "My bae is a muthafuckin' man!"

"Get yo' ass on lil' girl!" KeKe laughed. "Your ass don't know what a real man is!"

"Why wouldn't she?" Big Lee interjected. "Her daddy is a real man!"

"I can't tell the way you talk to him," Lay hissed and walked off from the bar. KeKe looked at her strangely then rested her gaze on Big Lee.

"What's wrong with our baby?" KeKe asked concerned. "She's had an attitude since she'd arrived at work."

"I don't know, child. She might be mad at Byrd," Big Lee suggested.

"I don't think she's mad at him, because of the way she kissed him when he came in here tonight. You would have thought that nigga had been out of town for months the way she tongued him down in front of everyone in here!" KeKe gossiped. Big Lee looked at the surveillance monitor and watched Lay and Byrd on one of the cameras. They were standing by the pool table, and it looked like he had a game going with

Whisper. It didn't look like Lay was mad at Whisper, but she couldn't understand why Lay was still mad at her. The way she just walked off and didn't respond to her statement let Big Lee know that her baby was still mad from this morning.

"Has your mama come yet?" Whisper asked, taking his shot.

"Yeah, she's over there," Lay replied smugly. "That's why I'm over here."

"Yo' ass still mad from this morning?" Whisper scoffed. "Y'all ass get on my nerves with that petty shit!"

"What you talkin' about, Whisper?" Lay asked with a slight attitude. "I ain't being petty. That's that lady's specialty!"

"And you're about to get your badge, shortly," Byrd added. "I can't believe you have an attitude with your mama because all mamas embarrass their children; especially in front of their girlfriends or boyfriends!"

"This has nothing to do with that," Lay insisted, feeling frustrated. "I want my mama to stop hiding shit from me. I'm about to be twenty-three this year, and up until recently, I believed another man was my father." Whisper looked over at her empathetically.

"I was mad at your mother for a while, and I still hold a bit of resentment toward her for not saying anything, but I love her big ass," Whisper offered. "She felt bad when you ran out the house, and she wanted to come find you to clear things up."

"I'm glad she didn't run outside to get me," Lay declared. "Because we would have gotten into a bigger argument. I just want to be mad at her, so let me because I am entitled!" Lay walked off and both Whisper and Byrd looked at each other.

"I ain't got shit else to say about the situation," Whisper scoffed.

"I ain't got no opinion on the shit, so it don't matter to me," Byrd replied throwing up his hands. Whisper picked up his bottle of beer and held it up at Byrd.

"We're going to get a long fabulously, son!" Whisper chuckled.

"I'm a quick learner, and let's just say I took a page out of your playbook," Byrd admitted. "I perfectly understand why you don't rock the boat with Big Lee, and it has nothing to do with you being a weak ass nigga. You are accepting of Big Lee's big personality, and it doesn't diminish your manhood when she flaunts it."

"I had to work really hard to get here because it used to bother me a lot. I had to sit down and have a serious conversation with her about the way she talked to me, and she came to an understanding that I am the man; regardless of how much she got in the bank. I used to think that as long as I was getting paid, it didn't matter if she talked down to me, or always snapped me up. However, one day I had a deep conversation with Deacon, and he helped me realize that Big Lee had me fucked up!" Byrd fell out laughing, and Whisper even laughed at himself. "Yo' ass laughing at me, but I'm serious. I told Ann I wasn't havin' that shit anymore!"

"And how did she react?" Byrd asked with a cynical look on his face.

"She got her ass in line! You see how her ass was moving on command!"

"She was doing what you told her to do," Byrd admitted, laughing.

Big Lee walked over and handed Whisper a shot glass. She handed Byrd the other one she was carrying and smiled. Whisper leaned down and kissed Big Lee on the lips then slapped her on the ass. Big Lee looked at him and smiled coyly, before she walked back to the other side of the bar.

Ew Baby was sitting at the bar and Big Lee came and sat down next to her. She hadn't had time to talk to Ew Baby about Cecil, so she figured now would be a better time as any. She reached over and grabbed her cigarettes off the counter. She took one out and fired it up, savoring the taste of the menthol.

"Ew Baby, there's something I've been wanting to talk to you about," Big Lee said solemnly.

"What's up, Mama," Ew Baby asked nonchalantly. She looked back at the door then down at her phone.

"Ew Baby, there's something I need to tell you. I should have told you this years ago, but I didn't know how to tell you." Big Lee sighed.

"Are you talking about Cecil being my father?" Ew Baby asked frankly. "Because Lay had already told me when she was mad at me. I wanted to come ask you about it, but I thought Lay was just making it up."

"Cecil is your father, baby, and that's why I took you in instead of letting you go to foster care. Lay begged me to let you stay, and I couldn't turn my back on you, even though I was pissed off at Cecil's ass!" Big Lee explained.

"I don't know how I feel about the entire situation. He had the opportunity to be a part of my life, but instead, he hid me like a dirty little secret. He should have reached out and told me instead of having you tell me," Ew Baby replied. "Patricia told me that one day I would find out the truth about my daddy, and I guess this was what she was talking about. I hate that bitch with every inch of my being, and I only hope and pray that she'll keep my sister's safe." The door of the lounge opened, and Ew Baby looked back to see who was coming inside. Ax walked into the door, but there was this light skinned woman who came in behind him. Ax spoke to everyone and the woman followed closely behind him. Ew Baby never took her eyes off of them and she was staring hard as hell. Big Lee saw how Ew Baby was very attentive toward Ax, and she hoped that didn't no shit pop off tonight in her place, because there was too much shit going on already! Ew Baby already had shit off the chain around here, and they didn't need anything else popping off!

CHAPTER TWENTY-EIGHT

$\mathcal{A}$x grabbed Angie by the hand and escorted her over to the other side of the lounge. He could feel Ew Baby's eyes burning a hole in his back, but he'd already explained the Amanda (Angie) situation, and he hoped that she would keep her cool. He knew that when Ew Baby was drinking, her attitude always was on ten. He looked over and locked eyes with Big Lee. She stared him down with the look of death, so he knew that if Ew Baby wasn't on one, his big sister would be the one to clown.

"Who is this?" Lay hissed with her nose turned up.

"Niece, be nice," Ax replied, widening his eyes at her. "This is Amanda. Amanda, this is my niece Layloni, but we call her Lay."

"Nice to finally meet you. I've heard so much about you," said Angie with a bit of nervousness in her voice.

"Oh yeah! Who's been talking about me to you?" Lay questioned. Angie was stumped, because she didn't mean to let that slip out of her mouth.

"I've been telling her about my very beautiful and smart niece, who's about to graduate from college very soon," Ax interjected. "I'm so proud of you, Lay, and I know that Cam would have been even prouder."

"Yeah, we talked about how we were going to go on a family trip when I graduated," Lay mentioned. "I went to see Tamara the other day to take her some food. Her stomach is getting big, and she's excited about the birth. Did you know that she's pregnant with a boy?"

"She's having a boy?" Whisper repeated. "That's awesome!" A sad look came across Ax's face.

"That's going to be my son. I'm going to make sure he doesn't have to want for shit!" Ax declared.

"That's going to be one spoiled baby!" Lay laughed. Ew Baby approached them with a tray in her hand. Lay saw her approaching, and the look on her face said that there was going to be some smoke in the city.

"Can I get anyone something to drink?" Ew Baby asked walking up. She walked in between Ax and Angie, mugging Angie up and down with her nose turned. "Who's your friend, Axel?"

"I'm Amanda, and I want a vodka and cranberry."

"What type of vodka?" Ew Baby asked smugly.

"New Amsterdam," Angie replied.

"She drinks that cheap shit," Lay uttered then laughed. "Do you really drink that shit?"

"Yeah, she drinks that shit," Ew Baby replied snidely. "Look at her... cheap is written all over her!"

"Excuse me?" Angie scoffed. "What did you just say?" Ax glared at Ew Baby with narrowed eyes. He saw that she was on some bullshit, and he'd better extinguish the flames before they rise.

"Ew Baby, go get the damn drink and cut it out!" Ax ordered. "You're making yourself look stupid."

"I thought you made yourself look stupid coming up in here with this bitch!" Ew Baby shot back.

"Am I missing something?" Angie asked with a smirk on her face.

"Naw, you ain't missed shit," Ax replied. "Ew Baby just don't take kindly to strangers and after my brother Cam died, she's been real extra with people she doesn't know." Ew Baby frowned her face up at him and rolled her eyes.

"Let that be the reason," she scoffed, walking off to get the drink. Ax looked over at Lay, Whisper, and Byrd then back at Ew Baby as she disappeared.

"Do you shoot pool, Amanda?" Whisper asked, trying to lighten the situation. He recognized the name, and remembered Ax saying something about fucking around with some new chick. However, he remembered hearing Big Lee say something about Ax and Ew Baby being a thing.

"I know how to play a little," Angie replied. "My brother tried to teach me, but I never really got good at it."

"Amanda's good at handling balls, though," Ax joked. Whisper and Byrd laughed, but Lay cut her eyes at him because she was pissed off, too. How was he going to bring some bitch up in the lounge, and he was just with Ew Baby this morning?

"I'm about to go to the other side," said Lay, rolling her eyes at her uncle. "Suddenly I feel like throwing up!"

"What's the matter, Lay?" Ax asked curiously. "Did Byrd Man knock one up in there?" Lay looked at him with an annoyed look on her face.

"Nope! I just don't like being around bullshit, that's all," she replied walking off.

"You let your daughter curse in front of you like that?" Ax asked firmly.

"She ain't cursing at me, so it really doesn't matter," Whisper replied nonchalantly. "You let your niece curse at you?" Ax looked at Whisper strangely as Ew Baby walked up with Angie's drink.

"Here's your drink," Ew Baby announced. Then she poured it out in front of Angie on the floor. "That's six dollars, Ax."

"What the fuck is your problem, Ew Baby!" Ax shouted. She looked at him like he had shit on his face then turned on her heels.

"Fuck you, Axel Wilson," she uttered before walking off. Ax looked back at Angie, who was amused by the entire thing.

"Ax, is there a problem?" Angie asked smugly. "I thought you said there was nothing between the two of you."

"Ain't shit poppin' between us," Ax replied. He looked over at Byrd who was staring at him. "I don't know what the fuck is her problem! Wait here while I go get your drink and a mop."

"I really don't need a drink, Ax," Angie insisted. "Let's just go someplace else."

"Fuck that! This is my sister's shit, and we gone hang here!" Ax walked off with a captive audience. Whisper and Byrd were quite interested in how Ax was going to handle it. He didn't seem quite himself, and they both noticed how he kept wiping his nose.

Angie was watching Ax with a bit of satisfaction. She had changed the pills that he kept in that small yellow envelope with some pure cocaine. She figured if he got high, he might as well snort the best. She started out the other day giving him a pill and pretended like she was getting them out of his pocket. She changed the entire content after she saw the effects, and he's been like a mad man ever since.

Ax came over and walked up to the bar. He stared at Ew Baby disapprovingly as she stormed across the room toward the back of the lounge. She had her jacket in her hand, so he figured she was going to take a smoke break. He turned and saw his sister glaring up side his head, because if looks could kill, he would dead.

"Why are you looking me like that, Lee Ann?" Ax asked defensively.

"Why you bring that girl up in here, and you knew Ew Baby was here working! I thought y'all had decided to give things a go, and here you are prancing up in here with some hoe!" Big Lee fussed. "You know that girl ain't all the way right in the head, and if she clowns up in my shit, I'm gone take it out on yo' ass!"

"Lee Ann, calm the fuck down!" Ax retorted. "I don't know why that retarded ass girl is acting this way! I thought we had an understanding, but I guess she wasn't on board."

"What type of understanding?" Big Lee questioned.

"That's none of your business, Lee Ann, so stay the fuck out of this," Ax seethed. "Ew Baby is a grown woman, and you ain't her mama for real!" Ax stormed off while Big Lee sat there in shock. Ax really went there with her, and she was stunned by her brother's behavior. She watched as he charged toward the backdoor then she turned on her stool to face the monitors. She wanted to see what Ax was about to do just in case she had to grab her gun to go check him.

Ax burst through the backdoor, and Ew Baby fell against the wall. It damn near scared her out of her skin because she was standing so close to the door that it almost hit her. Ax spent on his heels and stared at Ew Baby angrily. She didn't care if he was mad or not. She felt that Ax had no right to bring some bitch to the bar, even if it was Amanda aka Angie. He told Ew Baby all about his plot to keep Angie close to him. However, she felt it was very disrespectful to flaunt his hoe in her face.

"What the fuck is your problem!" Ax shouted, charging toward Ew Baby.

"What the fuck is your problem?" Ew Baby retorted back. "You're the one bringing bitches up to my job; being all disrespectful and shit!"

"I told you about that hoe, so I don't know why you're acting like this! I thought you trusted me, and the way you're acting, I can tell you don't!" Ax yelled. Ew Baby noticed a weird look in his eyes, and noticed he seemed a bit jittery. "I ain't goin' be deal with this type of shit with you, Ew Baby!" Ax wiped his nose with his sleeve then sniffed hard. He looked at Ew Baby and noticed she was looking at him strangely.

"What the fuck is wrong with your nose, Ax?" she asked suspiciously. "You weren't sniffing like that earlier?"

"Ain't shit wrong with my nose!" Ax seethed. "You're just trying to change the fucking subject!"

"Naw! I ain't trying to change the subject! Your ass look like you're high as hell, and I ain't about to be dealing with no dope fiend!" Ax grabbed Ew Baby by the throat and slammed her against the wall. He squeezed his hand slightly and applied a little pressure to her esophagus.

"Bitch! I'll fuck you up out here if you call me another dope fiend!" Ax grumbled angrily. Ew Baby stared into his eyes with same intensity because she wasn't scared of Ax. She knew that he wouldn't hurt her, because he would have to answer to Big Lee.

"You are a dope fiend!" Ew Baby shouted with conviction. Ax's eyes widened as his hand grew tighter around Ew Baby's throat. A smug smile came across her face as a single tear ran down her cheek. She lifted her chin and continued to stare into his eyes. Ax noticed she was getting off by his actions, and he felt his manhood strain against his leg. Ew Baby was a little freak and that's one of the things that turned him on about her!

Ax smashed his lips against Ew Baby's and parted them with his tongue. They kissed each other while Ax reached down and freed himself from his pants. Ew Baby pulled her leggings down, and he stepped inside of them. She latched her legs around his waist and leaned her back against the wall. He rubbed his stiffness against her wetness and thrust hard inside of her.

"Uhhh... hurt me, lover," Ew Baby sang as Ax continued to choke her. He pushed hard inside of her knocking her body against the cold hard brick wall. Ew Baby panted heavily as Ax fucked the life out of her, and she was enjoying every minute of it. She wrapped her arms around his neck and smiled greedily with every blow that he served. He was beating it up like a madman and Ew Baby wanted more. The passion and intensity of Ax's actions made her remember what it was like to fuck a man high on drugs. However, she wasn't signing on to deal with this type of erratic behavior no matter how much she loved Ax.

Big Lee stared at the screen and continued to watch Ax and Ew Baby. She didn't want to interfere too soon, but she didn't want Ax to hurt her daughter either. Whisper walked up to Big Lee, putting his arms around her, and he just so happen to glance at the screen. Both he and Big Lee jumped when they saw the two starting to have sex, and Big Lee turned away from the screen, because that's something that she didn't want to see. Big Lee looked back at the row of monitors and stared at the one with Angie in it. She knew exactly who the woman was at the bar with her little brother because she had several pictures of her, and even sat in front of her house and watched her from a distance. Big Lee wondered what was Angie's angle, and furthermore, what was going to happen when Cecil got out of jail.

CHAPTER TWENTY-NINE

$\mathcal{E}$w Baby woke up feeling sore from the dick down Ax had served her in the back of the lounge. He made her cum three times, and the one that came from him sucking her goodness almost made her bust her head on the wall. It was like an out of body experience, and he didn't want to let up. Whisper had to come out to get Ax because he'd just left Angie sitting in the lounge all by herself.

Ew Baby reached over and grabbed her phone. She hit the button and noticed she had thirteen missed calls from Dolly. A sudden panic came across her as she looked at the text message that accompanied the voice message. Ew Baby urgently dialed Dolly's number and hoped to God that her little sister would pick up the phone.

"Hello," Dolly stammered. "Ew Baby, where are you?"

"I'm at home, Dolly. What's the matter?" Ew Baby asked anxiously. "Did that fat fuck do something to you?"

"Please come get me!" Dolly cried. "Big Daddy's trying to have sex with me, and I think he hurt my mama!"

"What?" Ew Baby quaked.

Boom... Boom... Boom... "Open this muthafuckin' door!" Big Daddy shouted. Ew Baby heard what was going on in the background and panic came over her.

"Dolly, where are you?" Ew Baby shouted. She put her phone on speaker so that she could get dressed while talking to Dolly. "Dolly! Where are you?" Ew Baby grabbed a t-shirt off the floor and put it on. She ran over to the dresser and grabbed a pair of jogging pants out of it.

"I'm locked in my room, and I'm hiding on the side of the bed," Dolly explained.

"Do you have the bat I gave you?" Ew Baby asked anxiously.

"Yes," Dolly replied. "I... I'm really scared, Ew Baby! He hit mama real hard in the face and she fell to the floor!"

"I'm on my way, Dolly!" Ew Baby assured her. She was putting her shoes on when Lay came barging through the door.

"Why are you yelling, Ew Baby? What's wrong?" Lay asked curiously.

"That fat muthafucka's is trying to get Doll!" Ew Baby quaked. "I have to get around there before he does something to my little sister!"

"I'm going with you!" Lay fumed before running out of the room. She ran into hers and grabbed a pair of her New Balance sneakers off the floor. Next, she sat down and put them on quickly because time was of the essence. She was wearing a pair of SpongeBob pajama pants, and a tank top, but it didn't matter. She grabbed her hoodie off the chair and put it on, then she grabbed her hammer off the nightstand. "Come on, Ew Baby!" Lay yelled, but Ew Baby was already running out of the door. Lay ran down the steps and headed out too because they were going to fuck Big Daddy up, and there was no stopping them this time!

Ew Baby trucked down Aldine, headed toward her mother's house. Dolly was still on the phone and was terrified 'cause Big Daddy wasn't letting up on the door. Lay was right behind her with gun in hand, and Deacon just so happened to be taking out the trash when he saw her run pass his house. He called out her name, but Lay didn't even flinch. He hurried to the fence to see where she was headed, and when he saw Ew Baby a short ways in front of Lay, he knew exactly where they were headed. Deacon reached into his pocket and grabbed his cellphone. He dialed Big Lee's number, but she didn't pick up, and this pissed Deacon off. He called Whisper's phone, and he picked up on the fourth ring. Deacon wanted to start cussing, but he knew there was no time for any of that.

"Tell Lee Ann to get her big ass up and get the fuck down the street!" Deacon yelled through the phone. "Lay just ran down the street after Ew Baby, and she had a gun in her hand!"

"What the fuck!" Whisper shouted, running over to the backdoor. He threw it open and looked down the street, but his view was blocked by the privacy fence.

"Quit being nosy, muthafucka, and get Lee Ann! I think Ew Baby is about to kill Big Daddy, and Lay's going help her!"

Ew Baby ran up on the porch and grabbed at the door handle. Normally, the front door would be open, but today for some reason that wasn't the case. Ew Baby ran over and looked through the window, but she didn't see anything. She decided to run around to the back of the house because nine times out of ten that door was definitely open. Lay followed Ew Baby down the steps and around to the back of the house. They ran up on the porch, and Ew Baby tried to turn the knob, but that door wasn't open either. Ew Baby started to pound on it angrily while screaming obscenities at Big Daddy.

"Ew Baby, he stopped beating on the door," said Dolly anxiously. "Is that you outside yelling?"

"Yes!" Ew Baby replied. "All the doors are locked, and I need to get in the house!" The back door came open, and Ew Baby's little sister, Missy, was standing behind it crying.

"Ew Baby, he's trying to get Dolly! He went into the bathroom while she was taking a bath, and Mama hit him with the broom!" Missy explained.

"Where are Mama and the other kids?" Ew Baby blurted out. "Y'all need to leave this house right now!"

"Donnie and Jeff are over their friend house playing," Missy replied. "It's just me and Dolly in the house 'cause Big Daddy said we can't go nowhere!"

"That's because the nasty muthafucka was going to try to fuck y'all!" Ew Baby seethed. "I want you to run down to my mama's house and knock on the door. Tell her what's happening, and I'm gone go get Dolly, okay!"

"Okay, Ew Baby," Missy replied. She hugged her sister tightly around the neck then ran over to Lay. She gave Lay a hug as well then ran down the steps to go to Big Lee's house.

"You know we gone have to fuck his big ass up," said Ew Baby staring at Lay angrily.

"I got my shit right here, so what you want to do?" Lay replied. "You ain't got shit in yo' hands, but I got you all the same!"

"I'm gone grab a knife out of the kitchen and carve his ass like a Thanksgiving turkey!" Ew Baby raged. She walked into the house and looked around for something sharp to fuck Big Daddy up with. She ran over to the carving block and grabbed a large knife out of it. Big Daddy walked through the kitchen door and laughed because he was amused that Ew Baby had come to the rescue.

"What the fuck you want, bitch!" Big Daddy spat. "And what the fuck you think you gone do with that?"

"I'm finna fuck yo' big ass up, you big fat nasty, basement smelling bitch!" Ew yelled.

"You ain't gone do shit!" Big Daddy laughed. "And I guess you gone help her, huh, Lay?" He looked at her amused as well.

"Lay ain't got shit to do with this! This about you trying to fuck my little sister!" Ew Baby spat. "Lay, go upstairs and get Dolly!"

"She ain't going to get no fucking body!" Big Daddy declared, frowning at Ew Baby.

"Fuck what he's talking about! Go get my little sister!" Ew Baby demanded. Lay shook her head up and down at Ew Baby and headed toward the doorway. Big Daddy stood in Lay's way, and she raised her gun up at him instantly.

"I'll blow that hoof off your wrist if you try to touch me!" Lay thundered. "Now move the fuck out my way!" Big Daddy looked at

Lay and laughed. She pulled the slide back and aimed at Big Daddy's stomach. "Play pussy and get fucked if you want too!" Big Daddy studied Lay for a second and moved out of the way.

"You stabbed yo' boyfriend, so you'll definitely shoot the shit out of me!" Big Daddy stated. He moved over to let Lay by, but when she passed, he reached out and pushed her against the wall. Lay hit the wall and the gun fell from her hand. They both hit the floor, and a look of panic came across Ew Baby's face when she saw Lay lying there.

"You fat bitch!" Ew Baby shouted, charging toward Big Daddy. She jabbed the knife into his arm and twisted it, but Big Daddy backhanded Ew Baby across the face. She went flying backward and fell against the table. Big Daddy grimaced as he pulled the knife out of his arm and threw it on the floor. Ew Baby ran back over to the counter and grabbed another knife. She was determined to fuck him up, and if that meant getting her ass beat, then that's what was about to happen. "I ain't finna let you fuck up my sister life like you did me!"

"Ew Baby, you know you liked sucking my dick!" Big Daddy teased. "And the way you used to moan when I bounced you on top of this dick! I would love to put those little titties in my mouth again, for old time sakes!"

"I hate yo' ass!" Ew Baby yelled, charging toward Big Daddy again. She swung wildly scratching him on the arm, and he grabbed her tightly by her t-shirt. Ew Baby jabbed the knife into his hand, and Big Daddy slapped Ew Baby with his other one. Blood spewed from Ew Baby's mouth from the blow, and he came back across her face with another hard hit. He lifted Ew Baby up and slammed her down on the kitchen table. He was about to rip her t-shirt open when Whisper came running through the door.

"What the fuck is you doing!" Whisper shouted, and that's when Ew Baby grabbed the knife out of Big Daddy's hand and plunged it into Big Daddy's chest. His eyes bucked out at her, and he let her go. He stumbled backward, and Ew Baby jumped up off the table. She picked the other knife up off the floor and ran toward Big Daddy ready to finish fucking him up! She stuck the knife into his side and jabbed it repeatedly into his kidney. Big Daddy howled out in agonizing pain, as Ew Baby ripped the knife through his skin and tissue.

"You gone die today; you disgusting muthafucka!" Ew Baby yelled. "You ain't gone put that little ass infant dick in nobody else after I'm done with you!" Big Daddy fell to the floor while blood leaked out everywhere. It was like Ew Baby was possessed, and she took all of the years of hurt, anger, and pain out on him at this moment in time.

Lay lifted from the floor and saw Ew Baby covered in blood. She looked over at Whisper and Deacon who were just standing around watching. She couldn't believe that they weren't trying to help Ew Baby, so she jumped up off the floor and ran over to help.

"Ew Baby!" Lay shouted when she realized what was happening. "Ew Baby, that's enough!" Lay grabbed Ew Baby by the arm and pulled the knife out of her hand. Ew Baby looked up at her with a satisfied look on her face, and a sinister smile appeared out of nowhere. "Oh my God, Ew Baby! Is he dead?"

TO BE CONTINUED

ACKNOWLEDGEMENTS

I would like to Thank God for giving me this gift of writing. It is a blessing to be able to share my stories with you guys, and I appreciate each and every one of you that come along on my adventures! I would like to say Thank You and Welcome to all the new readers of Vivian Blue books!! It's a pleasure to make your acquaintance, and I hoped you enjoyed my story! I would like to thank my publisher, Porscha Sterling, for believing in me and giving me the opportunity to put my thoughts out here in the world!! I am truly grateful to you and the Royalty and Royalty Publishing House Family for all of your love and support!! I would like to give a Special Shout Out to Quiana Nicole and Michelle Davis for all of her help and support!! I've come to understand that you are a major gear in this crazy machine that keeps us shining, and I want you to know that I appreciate you! You guys are Black Girl Magic and along with P, I think of you as the "Royalty's Angels" Lol… (XoXo). I can't forget my AWESOME editor, Latisha Smith Burns, and her editing team at Touch of Class Publishing Services: "Where class meets perfection!" You are truly a gem, and I appreciate all of the love and support that you give me!! You get my oddness, and I am so grateful that you do!! To my test reader, LaShonda "Shawny" Jennings, thank you for your input and "realness!" You help keep me focused by keeping you focused, and I appreciate the love and support that you give me!! I am thankful that you are a part of my literary career because we go way back like Cadillacs!!! I would like to Thank, My Family for their continued support and love. You are My Foundation, My Rock, and there wouldn't be a Vivian Blue if it weren't for you!! To my readers, THANK YOU!!!! THANK YOU!! YOU GUYS ARE ROCK STARS, and I AM TRULY GRATEFUL TO YOU!! YOU'RE THE REAL MVP'S!!!! BE GREAT XoXoXo

PEACE, LOVE & BLESSINGS

Vivian Blue

CHECK ME OUT ON SOCIAL MEDIA

Facebook: Vivian Blue

Instagram: Authorvivianblue

Twitter: @VivBlueAuthor

My website: http://www.Vivianblueauthor.com

Amazon Author's Page: http://www.amzn.com/-/e/B0177JADR6

Facebook Likes Page:

http://www.Facebook.com/Vivian-Blue-3889021813110701

BOOK TITLES

*Torn Between Two Bosses: The Series

**Rise of a Kingpin's Wife: The Series, with a follow up:
Forever A Kingpin's Wife: The Series*

*A West Side Love Story: The Series

*Gangsta: A Colombian Cartel Love Story: The Series

*Friends Before Lovers, Standalone

*Love, Marriage, and Infidelity: The Series

*They Don't Know About Us: The Series *

*War of the Hearts: The Series

*She's a Savage for a Real Gangsta: The Series

*My Heart Is in Harmony by V. Marie
(young adult) Standalone*

Looking for a publishing home?

Royalty Publishing House, Where the Royals reside, is accepting submissions for writers in the urban fiction genre. If you're interested, submit the first 3-4 chapters with your synopsis to submissions@royaltypublishinghouse.com.

Check out our website for more information:

www.royaltypublishinghouse.com.

Text ROYALTY to 42828 to join our mailing list!

To submit a manuscript for our review, email us at
submissions@royaltypublishinghouse.com

Text RPHCHRISTIAN to 22828 for our
CHRISTIAN ROMANCE novels!

Text RPHROMANCE to 22828 for our
INTERRACIAL ROMANCE novels!

Do You Like CELEBRITY GOSSIP?

Check Out QUEEN DYNASTY!
Visit Our Site: www.thequeendynasty.com

Get LiT!

Download the LiTeReader app today and enjoy exclusive content, free books, and more

05816I762

CPSIA information can be obtained
at www.ICGtesting.com
Printed in the USA
LVHW032050081118
596444LV00016B/318/P